HER PONY EXPRESS HERO

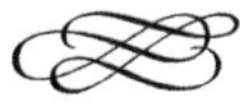

NIKI J MITCHELL

HER PONY EXPRESS HERO

Her Pony Express Hero
By Niki Mitchell

This sweet, second chance romance set in the Wild West will have you rooting for the hero until the very end.

A determined, courageous woman must choose between two good men. One ~~that~~ can provide for her. The other holds her heart.

When Chantilly Walsh's older brother is gunned down outside a Carson City saloon, she's determined to save her younger brother from the same fate and keep him safe. Wealthy rancher, Daniel Braddock, sets his sights on her—offering stability and security. Then the adventurous Pony Express rider, Blaze Steele, gallops into town and captures Chantilly's heart—until a terrible misunderstanding changes everything.

Chantilly is set to marry on Valentine's Day.

The only question is, which man will she choose?

CHAPTER 1

The distant snowcapped Sierra Mountains once brought Chantilly Walsh tranquility. Today they were silent witnesses to her grief and turmoil. Numbness filled her soul, walling off the wretched cold seeping through her threadbare coat and loosely knitted mittens.

A six-inch blanket of white smothered the flat ground where her older brother's coffin rested in the open gravesite on the outskirts of Carson City, Nevada. Empire Cemetery sounded grand. It wasn't.

Chantilly glanced toward the heavens. Dark ominous clouds threatened to snow more misery to this forsaken territory.

Her fourteen-year-old brother, Matt, had been

forced to grow up fast. His stoic face feigned bravado. If only she had the words to comfort him.

Boot steps crunch-crunch-crunched as the preacher took his place at the far end of the grave. He pulled up his leather jacket collar, tightened his knit scarf and cleared his throat. "Dearly Beloved." His breath puffed out like a stream of smoke. "We are gathered here today to pay tribute to James Marcus Walsh, our departed friend and brother."

Departed.

Dead.

Murdered at twenty-years-old on the morning after Christmas.

The impact of Jamey's death seized her stomach. Tears should be flowing, but she couldn't cry. She'd lost the ability years ago.

"Be assured that Jamey is worthy of redemption." The preacher folded his hands together. "He now rests with the Almighty Lord."

She peered around the site. Lots of folks came to pay their respects, even in such abysmal weather.

The sound of hooves pounded the ground along the snowy road to the north. A Pony Express rider kneed his horse and galloped toward town interrupting the moment of silence.

If she had her druthers, she'd much rather be out riding like the stranger.

The preacher sang "Amazing Grace." Others joined in. She mouthed the lyrics. Bible verses were quoted, but she didn't listen. Instead, she thought about her brother being gunned down outside the Silver Dollar Saloon.

The preacher motioned Matt to come forward.

Before he moved, she placed her hand on his shoulder and gave an encouraging squeeze. "Know what you're going to say?"

He nodded, stared at the coffin in the ground, and walked next to the preacher. "I admired my brother. He taught me how to be a man."

Matt and Jamey had been close. It saddened her that he no longer had a big brother.

Matt continued, "Must've been about seven when I stole a lollipop from the general store. When Jamey saw the candy in my hand, he marched me back inside and made me apologize. He was a good brother. Always watched out for me. He shouldn't have died."

Bile crept up her throat. She choked on old family secrets.

Matt stepped next to her, giving her a sympathetic hug. "Go on, sis. Jamey would want you to."

The pastor nodded.

She swallowed the hard lump in her throat and plodded forward. Emptiness filled her as she struggled for the right words.

In a withered voice, she lamented, "Brother, may you rest in peace."

Making her way back to Matt, she reached for his hand.

Sparky Miller, Jamey's right-hand man at the blacksmith shop, stepped up. His expression appeared as somber as Chantilly felt. "I considered myself one lucky fellow when I came to town three years ago and Jamey hired me. He had been an easy-going boss who loved to tell funny stories and jokes. Jamey died too young." He walked with his head down to the other side of Matt.

Their middle-aged neighbor came forward to speak. "Jamey might have liked to joke around, but I never once heard him say a bad thing to anyone. When my cane broke, he whittled me a new one." The woman held it up high. "What a special young man."

Jamey's best friend, Daniel, rushed next to Matt and Chantilly. "Sorry, I'm late."

"You want to speak?" Matt asked.

Daniel nodded and stood by the preacher. "Nobody could tell a story like Jamey. One that always ended with his infectious, hearty laugh. I'm gonna miss my good friend. May he rest in peace." He moved next to her and set his hand on her shoulder in a reassuring gesture. Too bad it did nothing to ease the dark emptiness threatening to consume her.

Several other folks came forward. They talked about

Jamey as a boy, talked about how he helped Pa, talked about the things he'd fixed over the years. She shivered wishing the preacher would speed things up.

"We are comforted that Jamey is now resting with the Lord. Ashes to ashes, dust to dust…" The preacher's humdrum voice droned on. He threw the first fistful of dirt on her brother's coffin.

An icy wind chilled her spine as she stared at the open grave, stooped down, grabbed the cold, gritty dirt, let it filter through her fingers onto his casket, and whispered, "What are we supposed to do now?"

Matt held his hand up and scattered two handfuls of earth on the coffin and mumbled, "I'll find the good-for-nothing lowlife who killed you."

Her heart stopped. Matt would not seek revenge, not if she could help it.

The service ended. Sparky said he'd see her at the shop on Monday. Folks gave hasty condolences and hurried for the shelter of their buggies or wagons.

Daniel's gloved hands held both of her mittened hands. "I'm here for you and Matt."

"Thanks." As far as the blacksmith shop went, she and Matt would run it with Sparky's help.

"Thanks for coming," Matt said.

"Of course. Anyway, I'd best be getting back to the ranch, but I'll be in town again tomorrow. Don't hesitate to send word if you need anything. Anything at all."

Daniel let go of his hold on Chantilly and looked directly into her eyes.

A chill flittered up her spine at his touch.

"See you tomorrow." Daniel tipped his white cowboy hat, drifted to his steed, and rode off.

Matt turned and embraced her. "Don't worry, sis. Since I'm the man of the house now, you can count on me taking care of you."

She held him at arm's length. "We'll take care of each other."

CHAPTER 2

Pony Express rider, Blaze Steele, galloped along the desolate road. He shouldn't be working on Sunday but the dang blizzard in Stillwater, Nevada, put him behind. He'd taken an oath to get the mail delivered on time and he'd done his best. On the trail since sunup, he'd paused only long enough to get a fresh horse. Snow kept up a continual flurry—not heavy although plenty annoying. Successful at completing his first two trips through this rough territory, his horse's steady hoofbeats kept him focused and urged him forward.

To the left, he saw folks gathered around a cemetery plot. What a dreadful day for a graveside service.

He curved right and continued on the Central Overland Route toward the distant city of Carson. Against the desert tundra, he made out the faint outline of buildings and storefronts. A man with a wagon full of hay traveling the other direction waved.

Blaze waved back liking how friendly folks could be.

In another mile, he made it to Main Street, slowed his horse to a walk, and rode by the two-story Silver Dollar Saloon. A brassy, red-haired lady of the evening leaned over the top balcony, and called, "Hey, Handsome. You must be the new driver everyone's talking about. Step in here, and I'll give you a welcome you won't soon forget."

He had no plans to visit but being polite, he said, "Thanks for the offer. Maybe some other time."

Her ruby-painted lips pulled into a pout. "If you change your mind, ask for Red."

Miners, cowboys, and businessmen lined the boarded walkways in front of the general store, assay office, and saloons. He continued past the blacksmith's shop and arrived at Carson City's Pony Express and Stagecoach Station.

The livery man came out of the barn. "Any trouble getting here?"

Quickly dismounting, Blaze lifted the heavy mochila bag and handed it to Jed. "Snow slowed me some." He unstrapped his saddle and put it on a wooden stand. "Nothin' I couldn't handle."

The man's expression turned sullen. "Reckon you rode by the Walsh's funeral."

"I did. Who passed?" With the chilly wind blowing, Blaze pulled up his collar.

"Jamey Walsh."

"Jamey died? I can't believe it." It felt like a rock dropped into the pit of his stomach. "I went to school with him." When times were simpler, before Blaze's ma died, and his dad lugged him and his brother to Sacramento in search of gold.

"I remember you two with Chantilly trailing after."

At first, she'd acted like a pesky little sister, but as she got older, Blaze formed a secret crush on her. Not that he ever said anything. After all, he'd just been a kid and embarrassed. He shook his head to clear his thoughts.

"Did you see Jamey when you came to town?"

"I meant to drop in on the family during my last stay, but I got in too late. Wish I could have seen him one more time."

"I know the feeling."

"Was it a riding accident?"

"Worse. The poor fellow got gunned down in front of the saloon. Nobody knows who the killer was. The sheriff's been looking for witnesses with no luck."

His childhood friend murdered. At twenty. The same age as Blaze.

"Gonna be hard on the kin."

"How's Tilly holding out?" Over the years, he'd wondered what had become of her.

"She's putting on a brave face."

"I'm not surprised. What about her pa? Is he still around?"

"Took ill 'bout two years ago. Died shortly after. Her only kin left is Matthew."

Over the years, he'd wondered what had become of her. Figured a purdy girl like her had gotten hitched years ago. "Is she married?"

"Nope."

Blaze wanted to shout *yippee* but didn't.

"Looks like they're here now." Jed gave a wane smile.

A carriage stopped in front of the stables. A lanky young man immediately hopped down from the left side. Jed offered his hand to help Chantilly down.

"Thanks for loaning us the buggy," she said.

"Least I could do after all you've been through." Jed turned to the young man. "How are you holding out?"

"All right," the young man said.

"Chantilly, Matt, do you remember Blaze Steele?" Jed asked.

"I can't believe you're here." Her lips quirked up at the corner. "It's been years." Chantilly threw her arms tightly around him. "How have you been?"

"Not bad. I'm a Pony Express rider now." Holding

her close, he breathed in her light floral scent… until she stepped back.

Blaze fixed his focus on her as she adjusted her hooded cloak around her head. Her pretty green eyes fringed with dark lashes reminded him of a lush meadow in the springtime. Eyes that used to dance in delight as she ran alongside him and Jamey on their way to school.

But today she'd lost her sparkle. She seemed to be keeping herself as strong as the fist she clenched at her side. Her mouth stayed grim, like she might crack if she allowed herself to think about burying a loved one.

Still, he stood there mesmerized, unable to speak, staring at the striking beauty. Her wide bow-shaped mouth tinged to a slight shade of pink from the cold. Memories flooded his mind. Memories of a spirited girl. A girl who always held a soft spot in his heart.

"Don't recall seeing you before," Matt said and eyed him sideways.

"That's because you were about five the last time I saw you."

"Well, I'll be fifteen in a few months." He puffed up.

Chantilly shivered. "As wonderful as it's been seeing you again, it's cold. We'd best get going home."

"How 'bout I take you and Matt out for a hot meal? My treat."

"It's been a long day."

"Come on, sis. I'm hungry enough to eat a saddle blanket. Besides, I've read 'bout the Pony Express and wanna see if the stories are true."

Blaze almost chuckled at the squeak in Matt's voice.

"Besides, we haven't been to Abbigail's in forever."

"You'll save me from eating alone." A strange sort of desperation grappled at Blaze's chest. He longed to spend more time with her.

"I suppose we could go." She turned to Jed who now wore a brimming smirk. "Thanks again for the use of the buggy."

"You're more than welcome." He pointed to Blaze. "Take good care of the little lassie."

"You have my word."

CHAPTER 3

Blaze offered his arm. "Shall we?" Once she took his elbow, a pleasant charge seemed to buzz through his ears. He ignored his reaction and noticed how she'd grown to be about three inches shorter than him.

As a kid her small size didn't stop her from getting riled up-full of spit and vinegar. He'd admired her something fierce, especially because she wasn't about to let anyone show her up. Did she still have that cantankerous side where she put her hands on her hips and taunted, "You ain't never gonna get the best of me."

Now he had a chance to be reacquainted with this gal. She'd grown up and stirred a forgotten desire inside his heart. He placed his hand on her lower back as they walked a couple of blocks on the boarded walkway.

"I used to be friends with Jamey in school. Tilly, too, although she usually tagged along with us. Not that I minded." He hated seeing her solemn expression and thought about giving her a little wink to get her to loosen up, but they both were grieving, so he chose to be respectful.

"What I remember is how you dipped my pigtail into your ink well. Had to cut a few inches off the bottom." Her breath came out like puffs of smoke as they passed the assayer's office.

"Did you really do that?" Matt's eyes twinkled.

"Guilty as charged."

Near the bank an older couple strolled in the other direction. Matt nearly tramped on Blaze's toes as he scooted over to the right to give the folks room.

"Keep in mind I was only nine at the time. I knew better, but when Tilly's long locks landed right next to the well, I just couldn't resist the temptation." A memory of her on the teeter-totter floated in his mind. One where she seemed to be all legs and knees. Even then she had beautiful large green eyes that often flashed with determination. Yes, he had taunted her and tried to get her to react.

Her lips twisted up slightly. "Because of your stunt, I

got moved next to Sally. She talked so much I couldn't concentrate."

"I am sorry." He placed his hand over his heart. "I promise you'll be safe from ink wells now." They crossed the street.

"You're forgiven. It was a long time ago," Chantilly said through chattering teeth.

"It was." They marched up a few steps to the entrance of Abbigail's Diner, and he held the door open. A waft of warmth from inside hit him along with the scent of baking bread and meat roasting.

She started to remove her cloak.

"Allow me." Helping her out of her hooded coat, he hung it on a hook on the wall and added his heavy jacket. Two long tables adorned both sides of the room which was sparsely filled with a splattering of people. Their voices were a soft hum of chatter giving the room a comfy feel.

Chantilly moved to the far end on the right, and he pulled out her chair taking a spot near the wall. Matt sat on the other side of her.

He stared at her snowflake pendant hung on a simple chain. The same trinket he talked his mother into buying for her ninth birthday because back then she loved it whenever it snowed. She'd been so happy that day that she'd twirled in circles until she got dizzy.

A week later he moved away.

The owner strolled up and set down a basket of bread near Blaze. "My condolences. Jamey was a good man," she said to Matt and Chantilly.

"Thanks," Chantilly said, as Matt nodded.

The fact Jamey had really died hit him square in the gut. He'd never get to reminisce about old times like fishing, skimming stones, or even sweeping the blacksmith shop.

Abbigail's dark eyes contrasted her white starched apron and severe gray bun. "Blaze Steele, you were a boy the last time I saw you. How long's it been?"

"Ten years."

"I heard you're riding for the Pony Express." The owner said in a bubbly voice as she smiled.

"Yep. Just got my route switched so I'll be in town once a week." Allowing him to visit the place where he grew up.

"That's good news. Anyway, tonight I'm serving chicken stew."

Matt's face lit up with a goofy grin. "My favorite."

"If I recall correctly, Matt, everything is your favorite," Abbigail chuckled. "I'll be right out with your supper."

Chantilly took a slice of bread and passed the basket to Matt and Blaze. Each of them slathered their slices with orange marmalade.

"You get the name Blaze from dodging flaming arrows?" Matt asked.

"Nothing quite that noble." Blaze shook his head. "Must've been five or six. Seems I knocked over a lantern in the barn. Set the hay in the stall a blaze."

"That's funny," Matt let out a long guffaw. "You burn down the place?"

"Nope." He glanced at Chantilly. Their eyes held for a brief second. Hells bells. Seeing her desire reflected back, his pulse quickened faster than the legs on a dog chasing a wayward calf.

"Who put out the fire?" Matt asked.

"My pa grabbed a bucket, filled it with trough water, and doused the flame. They called me Blaze, so I'd never forget what I did."

"Got a nickname myself. Daniel Braddock calls me Ace."

"Ace. I like it." Daniel had been two years older and several feet taller than him. And arrogant as all get out. Figured because he had money, he could push others around.

"Daniel and Jamey were friends."

Really. The guy and his rogue buddies once got the better of Jamey and Blaze behind the watering hole on the shortcut home. But that was history. The man could have changed.

Blaze certainly had.

"Daniel owns the Double-B Ranch, the biggest spread this side of the Sierras."

"Rode by it on my way into town. It's still an impressive place." Blaze hoped to own his own ranch someday. If he lasted the year, his Pony Express job should earn him enough to fulfill his dreams.

"Daniel says I'm a natural with horses and promised to let me help him the next time he's breaking broncs."

"That's way too dangerous." Chantilly's lips pressed together.

"You're not my ma."

Her shoulders sagged. "I'm just saying Flynn thinks you've got a knack for helping all critters." She turned to Blaze. "He's the town's veterinarian."

"I like working with Flynn. It's kinda fun figuring out what's making the animals sick or assisting with births. Horses and people are similar in some ways. We have a lot of the same muscles. Did you know horses and people have just over two-hundred bones? Of course, we don't walk on four legs." Her brother puffed up as he spoke.

"I never consider the notion before," Blaze said.

"Flynn thinks I'm smart enough to get in a college or university. I might even study medicine."

Chantilly flinched for a second then covered her unease with a smile that didn't reach her eyes. "We'll find a way for you to attend."

"I'm needed at the shop." Matt scuffed the toe of his boot along the floor.

Abbigail placed bowls of steaming stew in front of them, and Blaze's stomach grumbled reminding him that he had little to eat since sunrise.

"Bet you love racing across the country." Matt talked in-between shoveling bites into his mouth.

"It's not bad. Just wish the weather would remember to cooperate." He didn't care for snow drifts. Come spring he'd face flooded roads.

"Have you been to any big cities?"

"I lived in Sacramento when I was about your age. I prefer a smaller town like Carson City."

"At least you got to see the country for yourself." Matt rubbed his chin thinking. "What happened to the last guy, Rowdy?"

"Rumors are the ghosts of Fort Churchill got him spooked." Blaze didn't know the true story. The only thing that mattered was he'd been tired of his Nebraska route and found himself grateful to be in Nevada again.

"You think spirits are out there?" Curiosity rounded the brother's eyes.

"Not likely." He figured when a man died, he either went to heaven or hell.

"Please give Blaze a chance to eat." Chantilly cocked her head to the right and looked at Blaze. Her features were soft and feminine like her name.

"I don't mind answering his questions." He took his last bite of stew enjoying the conversation.

Abbigail cleared their plates. "Give me a sec, and I'll be back with slices of spice cake."

"Yum." Matt patted his stomach.

"Do you still fish at our spot?" he asked Chantilly, wanting to get her mind off her troubles.

"Not for years," her voice came out wistful.

"Are you talking about where the river forks? Jamey took me there plenty of times. Great place to catch trout," Matt said.

"That's the one. Might try it out again come spring." Fishing had been a cheap mainstay for food before he joined the Pony Express. "Maybe you could join me and Matt?"

"We'll see." Her shoulders stiffened, and he wondered why.

With a plate in front of him, Blaze forked in a bite and savored the nutmeg spice. "This is delicious."

Matt belched his approval and threw his napkin on the table.

"We'd best head on home," she said.

Blaze stood and retrieved their coats and helped Chantilly into her cloak.

"Is your home still behind the livery?" He wondered if she'd ever moved to a different place.

"It is." They walked down the steps, crossed the

street, and moved up to the boarded walkway. "Thank goodness Jamey hired Sparky to work at shop right after Pa died. He'll keep everything going." She looked down at her hands.

"I'm sorry for your loss. Your dad was mighty patient when he taught the three of us how to shoe a horse."

"I miss him every day. It looks like I'll be applying the things he taught me in the shop now," her tone came out serious and kind of melancholy.

"I'll pitch in too," Matt spoke up as he moved in front of them to let another couple pass.

"You two seem to have everything managed."

"We do." Her teeth chattered.

They reached an alley and arrived at the front door of the house behind the blacksmith shop.

"I'll be in town next Saturday. I'd like to take you to supper again if you're willing." The wintry air nipped Blaze's ears.

"That would be dandy," Matt shouted.

"Maybe." She glanced sideways at him, but with only streetlamps lighting their way it was too dark to see her expression.

"I'll take that as a yes. Pick you up at sundown." He pulled up the collar of his jacket and sprinted off toward the boarding house.

CHAPTER 4

After all these years, Blaze's smile still set Chantilly's heart a flutter. The lanky kid she once idolized had become even more handsome. His eyes twinkled when he spoke of his adventurous job creating a tinge of jealousy inside her. How she longed for the freedom to travel rather than work on ledgers or toil her day away doing housework or blacksmithing. She should be thankful to have a profitable business and a roof over her head. Folding her arms, she told herself to quit dreaming the impossible.

Matt held the door open to the two-bedroom cabin behind their blacksmith shop. The fire had died down, and the room felt almost as frigid as the winter's night. She threw a few logs in the brick fireplace, watched the flames jump, and warmed her hands. "We're running low on wood."

"Don't worry, sis. I'll chop some tomorrow." Matt meant well, however, knowing him he'd get side-tracked, and she'd end up doing the task. Being the youngest, Matt usually finagled either her or Jamey to pick up the slack.

Except Jamey died.

Tears refused to spill. She must move on.

She thought about heating a kettle for tea but nixed the idea. Tonight, tea would not mollify her frazzled nerves. Nor would reading a comforting verse from the family bible. As far as she was concerned, God had given up on her.

Restless, she eased into the rocking chair and picked up a sock to darn.

Matt snatched one of his science books, turned up a lamp on the round table between them, and plopped into the reading chair. "What are we going to do now that Jamey's gone?"

"You'll continue your studies and help in the after-noon with Flynn like usual." Shivers climbed up her spine, reinforcing the truth. Never again would she see Jamey's face or listen to his goofy jokes that picked up her spirit. It wasn't fair that he died. Her chest ached missing him.

"I can do more. Jamey showed me how to forge. Think Sparky will mind teaching me more tricks?"

"I don't see why not."

"Wish I were good like Jamey at bartering. One time he showed me this fancy silver teapot and said he got it for fixing a wheel." A grin brightened his face.

Chantilly fought off a grimace. She recalled Jamey showing her how he'd exchanged it at the assayer's office for several silver dollars. Then he traipsed across the street to the saloon and lost it all. His penchants for cards rarely brought back winnings.

But their account should be solid. No need to worry.

She yawned. "I'm gonna call it a night." Passing the old bed with the lumpy feather mattress, she remembered how proud her Pa had been when he carried the wood frame into the cabin. But he had died, and now Jamey was gone, leaving her to watch out for her teenage brother alone.

The day caught up to her.

She sat at the vanity in her bedroom. At the moment, with her hair in disarray, she took out the silver brush that once belonged to her mother and ran it through her locks. Even her hair appeared lackluster. Gazing at her reflection, her skin seemed pale. Dark circles had formed beneath her eyes. Well, she had a trying day.

She got up and plopped on her straw-filled bed. Fluffing her pillow, she said to herself, "Tomorrow will be a good day."

CHAPTER 5

Yesterday's funeral must have gotten to Chantilly. Too edgy to get another wink of sleep, she might as well get up. Wrapping a thick quilt around her shoulders, she ambled to the kitchen window and pulled aside the curtain. Dawn shone brightly on the silhouette of a rider leaving the stables.

Blaze.

Smoky eyes that twinkled with mischief. An endearing smile that deepened with dimples. A fun-loving personality.

As a kid, she had a crush on him. In the ten years since she last saw him, he'd become a man. One who treated her with kindness. His wide shoulders spoke of a man who didn't shy from hard work. The kind of man she wanted in her life.

She'd had her share of suitors over the years. Luke, who lived on a farm and had brawny muscles. Hank, who now worked at the mines. Even Charlie from the assayer's office. Handsome with dark wavy hair and eyes the color of chocolate, he'd brought her flowers, held her hand as they watched a play at the Golden Birdcage Theatre, and shared kisses under the moonlit night. But when he got down on one knee to propose, she couldn't say yes. She wasn't in love with him.

Shivering as she rubbed her arms, the temperature had dropped inside. Adding some wood to the fireplace, she heated a pot of water for tea.

Restless, Chantilly ran her hand over the roll-top mahogany desk, grabbed the record book from a shelf, and sat at the desk. Jamey had her enter deposits and debits from time to time. But she hadn't done that for a month or two.

She flipped the ledger to December not in the mood to work on this. But it needed to be done. After adding receipts and balancing the books, she smiled. With fifty-seven dollars left and whatever jobs came in this week they'd do just fine.

"I'm hungry. What's for breakfast?" Matt plunked into a chair at the table.

"How 'bout ham and eggs? A neighbor sent us a slab along with a loaf of bread."

"Yum."

She put away the books and nabbed the frying pan to cook their meal. Several minutes later, she set down the plates with food. "Got much work this afternoon?"

At about noon, right after school got out, her brother usually helped for an hour or two at most. Then he'd been free to do as he pleased. The daily grind didn't fall on him like it did with her and Jamey.

"After I take the wagon to pick up supplies for the shop, I'll patch a shovel and a few pots and pans," his voice cracked just like Jamey's had at that age.

Jamey. Why did you have to leave us when we needed you most?

Chantilly sighed. All the wishing in the world wouldn't bring him back.

"After that's done, I reckon I'll see what Flynn's doing." Matt hugged her quickly and shot out the door.

She let out a long breath. The more time he spent with the vet the better. A few minutes later, dressed in denim pants, her father's old shirt, and boots, she entered their shop.

Inside the shop, she relaxed, thankful for the warmth. Jamey's leather apron hung on a hook. Her brother who had been a fixture—would never again wear that apron. Two years older, he had seemed so wise. Normally, girls didn't work in the shop, but she wanted to learn and begged him mercilessly. He gave in after Pa died. Stressing safety, he patiently showed her the proper way to heat steel and shape the metal using an anvil, hammer, or chisel to make horseshoes.

And that's exactly what she'd do today.

Sparky heated metal to an orangish red color. He dropped an object in water, and it hissed. "How are you today, Chantilly?"

"Well." Compared to yesterday, this day seemed better. Still, her heart ached something fierce for Jamey. She put on her brother's apron and tied the back. "I'll be working in the shop today."

"That's not necessary. I've got everything handled," his voice boomed.

"I have to do something."

"How 'bout sweeping the shop?"

"Sure. I'm more than willing to shoe any horses that come in." Mind you, she hadn't done many, but she could do it.

"I know you're worried about the shop, but I'm not going anywhere. I'll make sure we're a success."

Jamey had talked about making Sparky a partner but never got around to asking. It's time talk to Matt about offering Sparky half of the business.

"Howdy." Old Man Caruthers called from the doorway. "Do you have time to fix Buttercup some new shoes, Sparky?"

"Sure." He winked at Chantilly.

"Much obliged." The man scurried away.

She'd dealt with horses over time and learned to sweet talk animals, using tranquil tones to calm them. She tethered the horse, picked up the foot and trimmed the hoof.

"I'll make the shoes. It'll go a lot faster that way," Sparky said.

"Thanks." She could do it, but for now, she didn't mind the assistance.

He plunged a red-hot shoe in water. Its hissing made the horse jolt.

"Shh, Buttercup. No need to fret," she said quietly and rubbed the horse's flank. The animal settled. Her chestnut coat and mane were matted. If she had a spare moment, she'd give her a good brushing.

Jed walked up from the livery. "Blaze said to give this to you." He handed her a sealed letter with her name.

Her cheeks warmed. She slipped the letter into her pants pocket to save for later and shod another horse. What would Blaze say? Most likely, it's a reminder he'd be escorting her to dinner next Saturday. The idea caused her heart to thump hard and fast in her chest.

The day flashed by. Matt and Sparky put away the tools.

"Have a good evening." Sparky tipped his hat.

"You, too." She locked up and walked out the shop

door toward the back. Pumping water from the spigot, they washed up at the outdoor basin.

Matt beamed at her. "We had a good day. Earned three dollars and a loaf of bread."

"That's wonderful." A splinter of relief filled her. Life would continue.

Jed walked up and pointed to her brother. "Think you could check the shoes on my Morgan?"

"Of course." Matt dashed off for the livery.

Finally, she had a chance to breathe. She rushed inside her quarters, moved to her bed, and leaned her head back on her pillow. Her heart skittered as she broke the envelope's waxed seal.

Dear Tilly,

Thanks for having supper with me. Your pretty smile will stay with me while I'm on the road and keep me content until I see you next Saturday.

Yours truly,

Blaze

His sweet words had her pulse speeding faster than the wheels on a buggy.

She got up and spotted Jamey's hat hanging on a hook.

Matt thought the sun rose and set upon Jamey. If she had her say, Matt would never step foot in a saloon again.

She had to make sure that this brother went to college and made a good life for himself.

CHAPTER 6

Blaze rode fast along the desert road. He had slept little last night because he couldn't get Chantilly out of his mind. Even as a kid, she'd been strong and independent. He recalled the time she skinned her knee in the schoolyard. She didn't cry and refused his assistance to help her stand. When the teacher cleaned her wound, she didn't flinch.

Last night, he caught her biting her bottom lip. The poor thing lost her pa and now Jamey. Every now and then, he'd got her to smile. Even laugh. And when she did, her beautiful eyes shone.

He wished he could stick around another day, but he had a good-paying job. Good fortune had been on his side when he found the Pony Express advertisement pinned to a board outside the general store.

As he stared out at miles of barren land covered in white, he thought back to the Carson City ranch close to town where his dad worked as a wrangler. He learned to ride as did his brother. Life had been good. Even after a bronco threw his dad and caused him to walk with a limp.

Two months after he turned ten, his ma died. And everything changed.

Pa said it was time to try something new and took him and his brother to the Sacramento gold fields in search of their fortunes.

The fortunes never came. Over a year later, Pa joined Ma.

He still missed them both something fierce.

Blaze and his brother found work cleaning stalls in the stables. One day, a man from Marysville hired them. A few months later, they were breaking horses. His brother married a farmer's daughter, and Blaze set off on his own.

He never considered himself to be the marrying kind, but if he did, the gal would have to be fine on the eyes but not delicate like a China doll. Not afraid to get a little dirt under her nails. Steadfast and unwilling to allow difficulties to crush her.

Someone like Chantilly.

He kept on riding. A scattering of cabins lined the

hillside, and he could see buildings in the distance. A few minutes later, he arrived at the Dayton stop.

"Hey, Reggie," Blaze said as he handed off the mochila mailbag to the station clerk and hopped off his horse.

Reggie took the reins from him, unloaded three letters from the pouch, and added another two. "Nice weather today. Heard you took on Chuck's route. You get caught in any snow."

"It had been touch-and-go for a while right outside of Deep Creek, but I managed." He hadn't minded giving up a couple of days' rest to help a fellow rider and figured he'd earn an extra ten for his effort.

Reggie placed the mailbag on the back of the saddle and snagged the reins of a horse tied at the hitching post. "Here you go. Safe ride."

"Thanks." Blaze took off for Desert Wells. With the sun shining down on him, no snow predicted for several days, and a fresh mount. Life couldn't get much better.

Late on Saturday afternoon, Blaze's buffalo skin coat, covered by an oilskin slicker, kept him tolerably warm as he rode along Main Street in Carson City. He couldn't help whistling "Camp Town Races."

He'd survived a brutal route. Snow crystals intermitted with icy sleet and heavy snowfall created slippery roads and snow drifts. Winds whipped through the canyons. But he didn't mind the job—not at twenty-five dollars a week.

Passing Chantilly's place, he hoped to catch a glimpse of her. He aimed to come courting tonight if she'd let him. Saddle worn, he'd best get gussied up first.

Dusk settled against the horizon as he dismounted at the Pony Express station and handed Jed the mail pouch and saddle.

"I'd like a buggy for tonight. Think you can get one ready?"

"Got one returned an hour ago. Are you taking out the little lassie?"

"I hope to." Blaze didn't want to jinx tonight by saying more. "Which way's the barber shop?"

Jed gave him a knowing grin. "Down three blocks on the left."

Again, he found himself whistling. He'd get to see Chantilly tonight. Last week, he'd caught glimpses of the lively girl he used to know. The one that kissed a frog on a dare, boasted about hitting the most quail with a slingshot, and bragged how her stones skipped the farthest across the river. She held her own with him and her brother, determined to show the world how tenacious she could be. And whenever she did something spectacular, her face would light up like a brilliant star.

Tonight, his goal was to make her forget her troubles. Enjoy her company and see what developed.

The last rays of dusk streamed across the sky. A handful of people walked the streets. He strode past the furniture shop, land office, dentist, general store, and bakery. Then he spotted the red, white, and blue striped barber pole and entered the shop.

"Hello, young fellow," the dark-haired barber's flap-winged mustache bounced as he talked. "You must be the new Pony Express rider."

"Name's Blaze Steele." He shook the barber's hand.

"My friends call me Cut. What can I do for you?"

"Short and clean-shaven." Blaze sat in a red leather chair. The scent of talcum filled the air.

The barber clipped. Inches fell to the floor. Blaze kept his eyes on the beveled mirror watching Cut snip the back. Dipping his comb in a watery solution, he parted the middle and trimmed the sides. "Is this okay?"

"Just how I like it." Looking like the dandies he'd seen in Sacramento he hoped Chantilly would be pleased. But he knew so little about what had happened in the last decade. Only that life had dealt her a poor hand.

"Given more bitter days ahead, you might want to keep that beard for extra warmth."

"Not tonight." He'd prefer to be less straggly for

Chantilly. Had he been overthinking their outing? Maybe, but he wanted tonight to be perfect.

Cut dipped a brush in shaving soap, lathered Blaze's face, sharpened a straight blade on a strap, and with one stroke at a time shaved off his beard. "You look like a new man."

"I sure do," Blaze agreed, flipping the man two bits.

Once back at the hotel, he'd order a bath to wash away the rest of the grime. Then he'd take out the prettiest girl in town.

CHAPTER 7

Blaze knocked and waited for Chantilly. Then the door opened. Her eyes widened. Her mouth twisted upward. "Blaze? You got your hair cut."

"Yep."

"Something else is different." She smirked, tilted her head to the left and scrutinized his face. "Your beard's gone."

"Is that a bad thing?" Warmth filled his chest that she'd noticed he'd spruced up to impress her.

"Not at all."

"You look ravishing this evening." Her long dark hair flowed past her shoulders, but it was those expressive eyes that got to him. He thought about the charming little girl who snuck table scraps to his dog or followed Jamie and him to the fishing hole or livery or school. She had never been a nuisance. Not to him anyway.

As he helped her into her woolen cloak, and she set the hood over her head, he couldn't wait to spend more time with her. "Where's Matt? I thought he'd be joining us."

"He went out with friends." The corners of her mouth quirked up. Holy smokes. It was like an arrow of heat shot straight through his body. "Meaning you're stuck with only my company."

"Which is fine with me."

She rewarded him with a shy smile.

"Is the Warm Springs Hotel suitable for our outing?"

"It's new. To be honest, I've never been to that establishment."

"Then it'll be a first time for each of us." He hoped this would be a long line of firsts. "You ready?"

"It's awfully cold out for such a long jaunt." She took his arm. "It might be best to choose somewhere closer."

"I rented us a buggy." He led her next door to the livery.

"You didn't have to go to such trouble," she said as they approached the carriage.

"I don't mind one bit."

Jed came out of the livery. "Everything's set. You two enjoy yourselves."

"We will." Blaze helped her up onto the padded seat.

Since the carriage was open, he handed her a quilt and took his place to her left. Flicking the reins, the horse moved down Main Street toward the far end of town. Kerosene lamps lit the signs for the Silver Dollar Saloon along with Johnson's Dentistry and Extractions.

He should say something. Too bad moths seemed to clog his mind.

He drove past Russell's General Store. The First National Bank. Precious Metals and Assay Office.

Still, no witty line came to him. He glanced over to her. "You warm enough?"

"Yes, thank you. The ride is lovely," she sighed. "It's been years since you and your dad headed for the Sacramento goldfields. I take it you never struck it big."

"It wasn't for lack of trying. The conditions were awful. We spent the days soggy and wet while panning in the river. Then Pa caught the grippe. Me and Walt ended up fending for ourselves."

"Is Walt working for the Pony Express like you?"

"Nope. He's married and living on a farm in Oregon. Just had a baby boy."

"I take it you didn't like Oregon."

"It's okay. I could have worked at Walt's father-in-law's spread, but I wanted to make my own way."

"Always seeking adventure. I remember the time you insisted on crossing that old wooden bridge and a board gave way. I'm pretty sure my heart stopped when you fell into the West Fork River." She gave him a wry grin.

"The drop was rather shocking and exhilarating." And right cold if he remembered correctly.

"Jamey was relieved when you crawled onto the shore alive."

"Looking back, trying to cross was a lame thing to do."

"It's part of being young. I know I've done plenty of silly things." She canted her head.

"Like what?"

"Skipping school to go fishing." She flashed him a smile.

"Because you followed me and Jamey. When I came home with a big trout, Pa cooked the fish and sent me to bed without supper. Thinking back, I got off easy. Did your folks ever find out?" He couldn't remember.

"Nope. Still, I felt guilty and never played hooky ever again."

"Same here."

"Think you'll stay on as a Pony Express rider for long?"

"For another year or so. Then I'll have enough money to buy my own spread."

"And move to Oregon?"

"Actually, I'm leaning toward the Idaho Territory. But if the right property came up, I'm flexible."

"I've heard that part of the country is beautiful. Someday, I'd like to travel there." She glanced down at the floorboard.

"You will." And by golly, he hoped to be the one to take her.

"The farthest I've ever been is Virginia City. We got to stay at the Fairweather Inn. At fourteen, I thought this was pretty special."

"Did Jamey and Matt go, too?"

"They did. I got to have a room all to myself, while the men had to share quarters right next to me. Not long after that trip, Pa got sick."

"You have had a pretty rough go of it lately. I'm sorry for your loss." He'd been dealt his own share of troubles, but he wanted to focus on her.

"That's life. Pa used to say when life gives you lemons, make lemonade."

Blaze chuckled. "If I recall, he had plenty of interesting quotes."

"He did. Matt's just like him in that way. He makes me laugh."

"Good to hear." Parking the carriage in a dirt lot, he helped her down. Offering his arm, he escorted her up the steps and held open one of the hotel's double doors. They entered a lobby with polished wooden floors and upholstered chairs covered in red velvet.

Noting a coat rack near the entrance, he said. "May I take your wrap?"

She pulled off her cloak. He hung it on a rack, then added his own. Her belted skirt accented her small waist and shapely figure. Her eyes met his, and she smiled. His heart beat faster. Holy smokes, she was gorgeous.

"Welcome to the Warm Springs Hotel." A hostess wearing a long black dress and starched white apron strolled up to them. "Are you here to dine or secure a room?"

What would it be like to get a room with Chantilly as his blushing bride? Talk about jumping the gun. He wasn't even officially courting her. "We would like a table with a window view," he said.

"Yes, sir. If you two would please follow me."

"Of course," he offered Chantilly his arm, and she gripped it rather tightly.

They were led past at least a dozen tables covered with white linen. The lights on the massive chandeliers sparkled with glass-covered candles. He pulled out a chair for Chantilly.

"Margaret is your server. She should be with you shortly. The special tonight is veal cutlet." The hostess handed them menus and walked off.

"This restaurant is quite fancy." She unfolded the cloth napkin and set it on her lap.

"You deserve the best." He glanced at the menu. Over a dollar a plate this place was pricey, but Chantilly was worth every penny.

"You're sweet."

"Thanks, I think." He'd rather have her call him dashing or charming.

The young server's skirt swished as she brought out a basket of bread. "Are you ready to order?"

"I'm torn between the roast lamb and beef stew." Chantilly stared at the menu. "What would you recommend?"

The server said, "On a night like this, I'd go for the stew."

"Then I'll order the stew."

"Make that two." After cold days on the trail, Blaze would be happy with any hot meal.

The waitress scurried to her next customer.

"Did you have a pleasant week?"

"Yes. Thank goodness we have Sparky. He's such a good worker."

"Has he been with you long?"

"A couple of years. Jamey hired him after Pa passed. It turned out to be a good choice."

"That's great." He offered her bread from a ging-ham-covered basket and took a slice for himself. "Carson City is a lot busier than when we were kids."

"Since the silver mine opened, we've had more business. Tell me about your routes. Any problems this week?"

"Not a one. No horse losing a shoe. No snowstorms. The sun shone most days." He put his hand on top of hers, surprised at how tiny her fingers were compared to his.

The server brought out their stew, and they nodded their thanks.

"You seem to like your job." She slathered butter on her bread.

"Most of the time." After all, it was just a job. A means to an end. "Do you still sketch? If I recall, you were pretty good."

"Once in a while. Lately, life seems to get in the way." She let out a wistful breath. "Enough about me. I remember you lost your mom right before you left for California."

"When Ma died, it seemed to take the thunder out of Pa." His words choked out. "If only we had stayed here. He might still be alive."

"Things don't always turn out like you plan."

He suddenly remembered the gift and fished it out of his pocket. "I found this at the outpost in Buckland's Station and thought of you."

Carefully pulling off the tissue wrapping, her eyes widened. "A handkerchief. My, it's the finest lace I've ever seen. Blaze, it's too much."

"But it's Chantilly lace. Intricate and beautiful like you."

She turned her gaze away and focused on a landscape painting above where they sat. Avoiding eye contact with him proved she was still shy about compliments.

"Consider it a gift between old friends." He might have overstepped by giving her a gift on their first official outing, but he didn't care.

"In that case, I suppose it'd be okay," she whispered.

"Good."

Her cheeks pinkened. "Your job's pretty dangerous, right?"

"No more dangerous than melting metal in a blacksmith's shop."

"The heat is controlled." She flipped her dark hair flowing past her shoulders in a sassy manner.

"Touché. Anyway, I'm careful." Except for galloping for hours at a breakneck speed or being drop-dead tired and falling off the horse, it was fairly safe.

"A part of me is jealous. You've traveled to so many places." She picked up her spoon and ate from her bowl.

"Where would you like to go?"

"San Francisco. From what I've read it sounds so exciting."

He rubbed his chin. "Then I'll have to escort you there someday. I can see it now, you in the finest gown twirling an umbrella. Me in a long coat and top hat strolling along the wharf with you, watching the ships come into the harbor, or taking in a show at a fancy opera house."

"That's a bit farfetched."

"There's no harm in dreaming." He looked directly into her eyes. "For the time being, I'm quite content to be with you right here."

"You've always been a charmer."

"I do my best." He reached for her hand. "I know you're in mourning, but when you're ready, I'd like to court you."

Her posture stiffened as her cheeks flushed. "I'll think about it." She gave him a coy smile.

All right. She hadn't flat-out said no.

"Remember when you left a toad on the teacher's desk, and she sat you in the dunce corner." Her lips quirked into an impish grin.

"Worth every minute, especially when the toad jumped clear on top of Miss Smith's head, and you let out a long belly laugh."

"You've always been a rascal, Blaze Steele," she said.

"Guilty as charged." He ducked his head and finished the rest of his stew. "Think it'll snow tonight?"

"It better not. I'm tired of being cold."

"So am I. I don't recall such a frigid winter. My last

run nearly froze off my toes. I heard Los Angeles is always sunny. Hope to visit the town someday."

"Another California town that sounds like a dream," her tone came out wistful.

And darn if he didn't want to make every one of her dreams come true. "I'm sure you'll get there someday."

"Maybe. Right now, I've got my hands full with the shop. You know, I started balancing ledgers when I was twelve. Times were simpler back then."

"I remember you were as smart as a whip in school." She often finished her lessons and then helped the little ones with theirs.

"I've always been interested in learning. Lately, Sparky's been showing me how to fix shovels and axles. I don't mind helping in the back."

The waitress came up to them. "Would you care for pound cake drizzled with caramel sauce?"

Chantilly watched Blaze.

"Yes. One for each of us. And two cups of coffee, please," Blaze added, knowing the heat would help ward off the chilly night when they left.

The server bustled off.

"Have you ever had a pet?" He didn't recall a dog in their household.

"I had a cat named Whiskers who was sweet along with being a great mouser."

If she liked cats, he'd have to find her a kitten.

"Your dog Sam was quite a character. I remember him sitting in front of a gopher hole, howling for hours, but he never caught the pesky rodent."

"Jamey said he must've had cow dung for brains."

"Sounds like him."

"Sam might have been dumb, but I loved my dog." His heart hurt something awful when he left Sam behind with one of the buckaroos at the ranch where his father had worked.

The server dropped off the cake. She sampled a bite. "This is delicious."

"It sure is. My mouth waters remembering your ma's pies. Did she teach you to bake?"

"I can cook but my desserts never turn out as tasty as hers."

They finished their meal, and he paid the bill. The ride back to her place seemed comfortable.

He helped her from the buggy and walked her to her door. "I hate for the evening to end. Wish I didn't have to deliver an important message tomorrow." He sighed, then plunged ahead. "I heard there's a dance next weekend and would love to escort you."

"We'll see."

He couldn't resist running his thumb along her chin and forcing her to look up. Without hesitation, he said, "See you Saturday."

CHAPTER 8

As the sun peeked through the windows Friday morning, Chantilly peeled open her eyes. Eyes that felt like she had rubbed them with sandpaper.

Mercy, she was tired. All thanks to Matt.

Last night, he came into the cabin drunk as a skunk singing a bawdy version of "Camp Town Races" and woke her up from a sound sleep.

When she looked into his room, she found him face first on his bed snoring. Sound asleep.

Hells bells. She didn't even get a chance to yell at him. Probably for the better. She doubted he'd remember a thing.

But that didn't stop her from tossing and turning and worrying about her brother.

She got dressed and stomped into the kitchen,

added wood into the bottom of the cast iron stove, and banged the fry pan on top of the burner. Whisking ingredients together to make biscuits, she punched the dough twice before rolling it with a heavy hand and using a cup to cut out several round circles.

If Matt thought she'd watch him follow in their brother's footsteps, he was an insipid fool.

She set the tray into the oven and slammed the door shut. The action did nothing to appease the worry twisting her stomach in knots.

Placing strips of bacon into a pan, she listened to them sizzle. The sound matched her mood. Sizzling mad.

The door to Matt's room opened, and he plopped into a chair. His eyes had a tinge of red in them. "Good morning."

"Is it?"

"Sure. Are you mad about something?"

She flipped the bacon. "Yep."

"Don't be. I just had fun with my friends."

"Good for you. Who cares if you woke me up?"

"Sorry," he shrugged, not at all chagrined.

She pressed her lips together as she added the crispy bacon onto two plates and used the grease to make gravy.

"Don't be like this," his tone came out soft and pleading.

"I know I can't tell you what to do but getting bashed, on a weekday no less…" She held her breath.

"Like I said. We were just having a little fun."

"In a saloon?" She had to ask. Toward the end, Jamey spent most nights drinking and gambling. An image of throwing dirt on his casket came to mind, and she shuddered.

"I'm plenty old enough. 'Sides, Jimmy's dad was there.'"

The idea of what he'd done had her stomach roiling with angst. "You're all I've got. I don't want you to end up like Jamey." She couldn't lose him.

"I won't. I promise."

If only she could protect him from the hard cruel world. She took the biscuits out of the oven, added several onto two plates, covered them with gravy, and set down both plates at the table before joining him.

They ate in silence. Matt finished his meal and put his dishes into the sink. "Gotta go. See you at the shop later." And he went out the door.

Her internal thoughts said the two of them had to get the heck out of this town before it ruined another brother. With her head down on the table, she breathed in slowly, allowing her angst to somewhat subside. Then she headed into the shop.

Grabbing an apron from a hook inside the stone building, she walked into the blacksmith station. It might be nippy outside, but the metal roof kept the weather out while the furnace kept the room toasty warm.

Sparky set a glowing horseshoe on an anvil and pounded it.

She grabbed a broom and swept the back of the shop. Her thoughts drifted to Matt. There had to be something she could do to keep him on track.

If only she had the money to send him away to college. Since she'd done the books for the business the past five years, she understood finances. The shop did well enough to support them with a bit of extra money for clothes and necessities.

Knock it off. Think of something positive.

In another few months, it would be spring. Then summer. Her favorite season with plenty of sunny days and beautiful butterflies.

She loved how carefree the insects were as they flittered around doing their own personal happy dance. She danced as she swept the floor.

Sparky cleared his throat.

She startled and her face heated. Darn, she'd been caught dancing with a broom.

"Didn't mean to disturb you." He chuckled. "You wanna help me make Prissy some shoes?"

Sparky pointed to a plow horse tied up at a post.

"Sure. I'll heat the steel." She put on thick gloves and set several rods in the fire.

She loved being useful. Productive. Busy.

"Mind if I give you a couple of tips?" Sparky asked.

"I'd like that."

"The secret is to get the steel good and hot and malleable."

How many times had she heard her pa say the same thing?

"Let it get really red in the hearth. Give it another minute or two." He handed her a pair of tongs.

In no time, she shaped the metal with a fuller.

"Make it good and round. That's it." Sparky encouraged her as she pounded the metal, put it back in the fire, and hit it again.

"You're doing great." He spoke in a steady tone.

"Thanks." She dropped the shoe into water, and it hissed.

When she pulled the cool metal out, she checked the fit on the horse. Perfect. Then she made the other three shoes.

Thank goodness she had Sparky here. This shop wouldn't survive without him.

"Are you going to the shindig tomorrow night?" he asked as she created another shoe.

"Yes." She thought of Blaze. Tomorrow night she'd

see him again. Being around him lit a spark of lightness in all the recent gloom.

"Wouldn't miss it. Miss Sally already promised me the first dance." Sparky's face broke into a big grin.

"You sweet on her?" Since Sally moved to town last month, he'd been seeing her.

"I reckon."

"I'm gonna take a break." Done with her tasks, she took off her gloves, headed outside, and plowed right into a solid body.

"Chantilly, what's the rush?"

She cricked her neck and gazed into Daniel's eyes bluer than Lake Tahoe. "Just getting some air."

Tall and muscular and handsome, she'd overheard women saying they'd set their cap on him. Plenty batted their eyes at him, and he'd flirted right back. But to Chantilly, he was just a friend.

"How you holding out?" He took her hand in his.

"Besides missing Jamey I'm doing fine." For the past week, she had gone through her days in a trance, plugging away as each second ticked by.

"Let's sit over there. I've got something that might cheer you up a bit." Daniel led her to a bench in front of the shop's building. Once seated with him next to her, he handed her a small bag.

She stared at the bag.

"Open it. I promise you'll like it."

She pulled out candy in a wrapper. "Taffy. You're sweet." She plopped the sugary goodness in her mouth and sighed.

"Just acting neighborly. I am wondering if you're going to the dance."

"I am."

"How about I bring my buggy before sundown to take you and Matt?" He put his hat in his hands. "I'll even let him drive if he'd like."

"Thanks for the offer, but someone else is escorting me."

A grimace graced his mouth for maybe half a second, but it was quickly replaced with a twitch of his lips upward. "Well, at least promise me a dance."

One dance with a friend of the family wouldn't hurt. "Okay."

"I'll look forward to it." He took her hand in his and kissed the top. "See you soon."

As he strutted off, her skin prickled along the back of her neck. She shook the crazy reaction off.

CHAPTER 9

Saturday after Chantilly closed up shop, she opened her wardrobe and sifted through her dresses, wanting to look pretty for Blaze. She pulled out her yellow chiffon and decided it looked more like a summer gown. The brown one with bric-à-brac seemed too plain. The long-sleeved navy one had seen better days. Fingering the flowered gown she'd worn when she accompanied Blaze to the hotel, she let out a sigh. No way would she wear that one again.

If only she'd taken the time to find a new dress in town. Still, buying something that she would rarely wear would be frivolous.

Eyeing the keepsake chest at the bottom of her bed, she thought about her mom. After she died, her things were folded inside a chest and brought into her room.

Thinking back, she figured Pa had done that because any reminder of his wife made him sad.

Over the years, Chantilly would occasionally look through the trinkets, ribbons, and knickknacks in a box near the top. A few times she'd tried on the gowns that were huge on her slight frame, picked up the sides of the skirt and danced around her room.

Curious, she opened the chest, set a patchwork quilt on the bottom of her bed, and removed the lid, fingering an embroidered handkerchief with her ma's initials. Then she came to a yellowed christening gown. A baby's locket. A hand-painted miniature picture of her mom. A few skirts and blouses. She held them up to her. They looked like they'd fit so she set them on her bed.

Her fingertips glided against a soft emerald fabric. Holding the material against her body, long sleeves belled in three flounces and complimented the fitted bodice. The floor-length gown had a full underskirt. This must be the fancy dress her mother spoke about wearing when she was seventeen and first met her dad.

Looking up toward the ceiling, she felt as if Ma were smiling down from the heavens and telling her to try it on. Just a smidge loose in the waist, the rest of the gown fit well. She twirled around the small space, feeling whimsical and happy.

Brushing her hair up in a loose chignon, she looked

in the beveled mirror above the lowboy dressing table and nodded in appreciation.

The clock chimed to the half hour. She had a few minutes to relax and pulled out the letter from a drawer Blaze left for her last Monday and reread the words.

CHANTILLY,

The lively girl I remember has turned into a beautiful lady. Keep me in your thoughts as you will be in mine. I will count the days until the dance and a chance to hold you close.

Best regards,

Blaze

HER PULSE SPUN FASTER than wool on a spinning wheel.

Blaze.

Full of adventure. Full of lively stories. Full of promise.

She'd never have guessed the boy she'd once punched in the nose would grow up to be such a romantic. In a few minutes, she'd be seeing him.

The grandfather clock chimed six times. She tucked the note inside her dresser drawer. Matt knocked on her door, and she opened it.

"You buy a new dress? It's nice." Her lanky brother

towered over her. Handsome, with dark hair and hazel brown eyes, he was the spitting image of Jamey.

"It belonged to Ma."

He eyed her from top to bottom. "I barely remember what she looked like." Her brother had been only six when she passed.

She flipped through the chest and pulled out a miniature portrait. "This is Ma as a young girl."

Matt held the object close. "You look like her."

"Pa used to say I had her hazel green eyes."

"I recall her singing when she cooked. What else did she do?"

"She loved to embroider. She tried to teach me, but I never got the knack." Chantilly's eyes misted.

"At least you're good at darning socks."

"That's out of necessity."

"Are we going in a buggy with Jed? It's as cold outside as a cow giving icicles instead of milk."

She let out a loud guffaw. "Where do you come up with such lines?"

"Just plum come to me." He gave her a lopsided smile.

"You're one in a million." She almost ruffled the hair on the top of his head like she'd done countless times as he grew up but stopped herself. Matt wasn't that little boy anymore. "Anyway, about the buggy. We're going with Blaze."

"Good."

Knuckles sounded against her door.

Butterflies flitted around her stomach.

"Howdy, Blaze. Did you run into any trouble delivering the mail this week?" Matt asked.

"I spotted a pack of wolves in the foothills near the California border but they didn't pay me much mind." Blaze strutted inside wearing a new black Stetson that made his warm cinnamon-brown eyes sparkle. His intense gaze danced tingles up and down her arms. "Tilly, I swear you're even prettier than the last time I saw you."

She told her heart to stop beating so fast, but it wouldn't listen.

"We're getting a buggy from Jed." Blaze turned to her brother. "You wanna drive?"

"Sure." Matt rushed out the door.

"Love his enthusiasm." Blaze gave her an endearing grin.

CHANTILLY ENTERED the Carson City Inn through the spacious foyer and had a clear view of the ballroom. The elegance of high ceilings, polished wooden flooring, and crystal chandeliers took her breath away.

The din of a couple of dozen people all dressed in

their Sunday best made her smile. Folks in Carson City sure took pride in their dances.

"May I take your cloak?" Blaze asked.

"Yes, please." Jackets filled the hooks nailed to a long wooden board on the wall. He added hers to the others.

"I see my friends over there." Matt pointed to a group of about six or seven teenage boys. Most of whom she'd known for years. Still, as Matt rushed toward them, the idea that her brother came home drunk after carousing with these boys left her with unsettling feelings.

"Your dress makes your eyes a deep green."

Blaze's comment distracted her out of her unpleasant thoughts. "Thank you." She glanced toward the entrance. Daniel strolled in. Spit shined and swanky. His dark waistcoat and matching Stetson gave him the look of a dapper gentleman. For all sense of propriety, he fit the bill, being a prominent landowner in the region. The coy looks several of the ladies in the room gave him said many of the young available women sought his attention.

Daniel tipped his hat in her direction. Then he walked over to the assayer's daughter, Juliet, a dark-haired beauty, and took her hand.

Chantilly wondered if they were courting.

On a raised platform at the far end of the room,

three cowboys—their musicians for the night —warmed up.

"The place hasn't changed much," Blaze said. "I wonder if my initials are still carved in the privy."

"You really did that?"

"Not just me, Jamey too."

She tilted her head. As youngsters, they were often causing mischief.

"Honestly. We were only ten. Had to do a little something to liven up the night." His eyes lit with his smile. Dang if her heart hadn't gone plum loco. "Then I asked you to dance. Doubt if anyone ever caught on to me and Jamey."

"And here I thought you liked me. Now I realize I had been just a ploy in your scheme." She couldn't help giggling.

"I did like you." He chucked his thumb under her chin forcing her to look directly at him. "But no way could I admit it out loud. Jamey would have teased me mercilessly."

"Welcome folks." the caller said. "I hope you're ready to kick up your heels. Grab your partner for the 'Beer Barrel Polka.'"

Blaze walked her to the center of the floor, positioned his left arm below her shoulder blade, and grasped her right hand. His touch shot tingles throughout her body and made her cheeks warm.

The fiddler swiped his bow across the strings, and they danced across the floor as a banjo strummed, keeping the music lively.

Blaze spun her under his arm and jigged on with the polka. "Are you enjoying yourself?"

"I am."

A couple stepped into their pathway, and he made a sharp right causing her to step on his foot.

"Guess I'm not the only one having trouble concentrating," Blaze said with a cheeky tone, tugging her closer.

"It's your fault."

"If you say so." He laughed reminding her of the boy she knew.

"Admit it. You're still a rascal."

"What I'll admit is I'm the envy of every man in this room." His deep voice combined with his closeness tantalized every fiber of her being.

What a charmer. She might have swooned if he hadn't been holding her.

Then the song ended.

The caller instructed the guests to form a square with three other couples for the "Texas Star."

To her right, Daniel stood with Juliette and nodded at her.

Chantilly was happy to see her brother's friend and smiled politely in return.

"Ladies, meet and greet," the caller's voice boomed from the stage.

She walked to the center, clapped her hands, and sauntered back.

"Love how that dress swishes." Blaze's eyes twinkled.

"Wave to your own and pass her by—catch the next girl on the fly—star promenade," the caller yelled.

Blaze passed her to the banker who gave a brief nod. "Miss Chantilly."

"Hello." She lifted her palm "star up" to meet his hand.

"Scoop up your right-hand lady around the waist," the caller said. "Walk side-by-side in the Texas Star."

Daniel slid his arm around her waist. "You're looking mighty fetching this evening."

"Why thank you," she said.

"Is that fellow courting you?" Daniel spun her.

"Maybe."

"Well, I'd like to change your mind about him and have every intention of calling on you," his voice came out so low that only she could hear.

Come calling? That was a first. Daniel never really paid her much mind when Jamey had been around. Women called him a catch. Still, nothing about him made her heart flutter or her pulse race like it did thinking about Blaze.

"Just so you know, I invited Matt and his friends out to the ranch. Seeing how much fun he had last time with the horses, I thought the trip might pick up his spirits." Daniel danced forward with her.

Daniel was a family friend. He would look out for Matt. Maybe visiting his ranch might stop him from following in Jamey's footsteps. "I'm sure he'll like that." As she said the words, she questioned if he was trying to win her over through her brother.

At least Daniel stopped all talk of courting. She strode forward to take Blaze's arm and danced around the square with him.

"Glad to have my gal back." His warm eyes reined her in. Hells-fire, the man could easily hornswoggle her heart if she let him.

BLAZE HELPED Chantilly into the front seat of the buggy, offered her a quilt, and took the reins. "I enjoyed your company tonight."

"It turned out to be an entertaining evening." She adjusted the blanket over her lap.

He flicked the reins. The buggy lurched forward, and he put his arm around her shoulders. "May I escort you to church?"

"Jamey used to take me and Matt." Her voice caught. "This will be my first time without him."

"I'm sorry." He wished he could take away that hurt.

"You're welcome to sit by me if you'd like." She glanced at him with an innocent invitation.

"I would. Think I could talk you into a picnic afterwards?" he asked.

"I can't make any promises."

They arrived at the livery. He helped her down and walked her home, her hand nestled in his. The simple touch made his connection to this lady stronger. His eyes darted to her face and that sumptuous bow-shaped mouth that he'd been dying to sample all night.

Would that be rushing things?

They reached her door, and she fluttered her eyelashes at him.

"May I kiss you?" She was in mourning. But heck, Chantilly had a way of totally distracting all sense of reason.

She nodded, and he wanted to shout, *Yippee*!

He leaned in closer, staring into her eyes which seemed to darken to a deeper shade. Pressing his mouth against the velvety fullness of hers a warm tingle shot through his body. He continued with a feather-light touch while doing his best to keep his response gentle.

She let out a little sigh.

He lifted his gaze as she opened those green eyes

and tilted her head confused. Her hand covered her mouth.

He wracked his brain to come up with something witty. Something to make her laugh. "Did you know your lips are sweeter than strawberries?"

"No, I didn't," she giggled.

He couldn't resist leaning down, pressing his mouth to her lips, and reveling in the softness before he pulled away.

Her cheeks flushed as she said, "Good night, Blaze," and stepped inside.

He whistled as he walked back to the boarding house. Life was good.

CHAPTER 10

Chantilly had tossed and turned all night reliving the fact that Blaze had kissed her.

She rolled over on her back, set her hands above her head, and let out a dreamy sigh.

His mouth grazed against her lips. Warm. Exciting. Sizzling.

And she invited him to sit by her at church.

She turned to her side. Was that wrong?

It's church. Everyone is welcome.

I'm just making a big thing out of a simple peck.

She closed her eyes and jiggled her foot.

I can't sleep. She pulled back the curtain to see the sky had already turned to dawn. *Get up and make some tea.*

She could skip the service. After all, she hadn't yet

forgiven God for taking away another member of her family.

Her mother would probably roll over in her grave given she believed Sunday worship was good for the soul. Her darn conscience told her to go. Thus, she made breakfast and got ready for church wearing her Sunday best, a blue flowered dress with a squared collar.

With time on her hands, she sat in a chair in the living room and picked up *Pride and Prejudice.* She adored the way Jane Austen described life for the English aristocracy. The balls, the fancy gowns, the ritzy lifestyle. Soon she got lost in the bantering between Elizabeth and Mr. Darcy.

Lost in the story, the grandfather clock's chime startled her. She stood and straightened out her skirt. Then she scurried out the door.

A light snow dusted the hills to the east of the shop. Property her pa had once said they'd build a house on before ma died.

She ducked into the alley behind the furniture shop and stepped up onto the boarded walkway. Peeking in the dentistry window, she glanced at the tray of tools. When she noticed molar extractors, she hurried her steps. The idea of having a tooth removed made her shudder.

Passing the general store on her way to church, the

owners joined her. "What a delightful morning for a walk," the woman said.

"It is." Chantilly found the air rather nippy but opted to be agreeable.

Near the hitching post, Blaze stepped next to her. A layer of stubble shadowed his chin giving him an air of handsome ruggedness. "Mind if I walk with you?"

"Not at all." Her face heated. She sucked in a deep breath, and said, "You remember Blaze Steele. He's our new Pony Express rider."

"Good to see you again." The husband shook Blaze's hand. "How've the roads been lately?"

"Decent for the most part, even though it's often right cold."

"This winter's been a bad one," the husband added as they stopped at the bottom of the church steps.

"It's been nice chatting with you." The wife smiled graciously, latched on to her husband's arm, and hurried up the stairs.

Blaze and she ambled inside the church and moved sideways into the second pew from the back. Surrounded by church going busybodies, their gossip about her and Blaze would be all over town by the end of the service if it wasn't already after dancing with him last night.

Did she care?

Definitely. She strived to belong.

The choir sang, "Praise the Lord, His Glories Show." Their melody came out in harmony.

The preacher gave his sermon, declaring with gusto, "Keep your mind devoid of immoral thoughts, lest you find your soul in league with the devil himself."

Breathing in Blaze's musky scent, she remembered his warm, tempting mouth. Heat spread across her cheeks as she squirmed in her seat.

This wasn't the place to have such thoughts bombarding her. Still, her lips tingled, refusing to repent. The kiss last night had been special.

The service ended, and they waited in line at the back foyer and inched along as they reached the pastor.

"Chantilly. Have a blessed day."

"I will."

"Heard you were in town, Blaze. It's been years." The pastor shook Blaze's hand.

"Yes, it has."

"Hope you'll visit our church again."

"You can count on it." With a parting nod to the preacher, Blaze offered Chantilly his arm and guided her along the boarded walkway. "Ready for our picnic?"

"It's too cold to be outside."

"Already got this covered. We're eating indoors."

"Thank goodness." She couldn't resist kissing his cheek.

Blaze pulled open the barn-style door and brought Chantilly into the carriage house. The structure with ten-foot rafters dwarfed his size. Dozens of buggies were parked on both sides as he led her through the middle and to a corner in the back.

Before church, he'd covered a haystack with a red-and-white checkered tablecloth. Thanks to help from the boarding house where he stayed, a basket sat in the center of the makeshift table with a jug of apple cider next to it.

"You did all this for me?" She sat on the edge of the haystack. "I'm not used to being spoiled."

"Well, get used to being pampered. I want you to know I'm interested. When you're ready I'd like to court you properly?"

"I believe I might be ready."

"Really." Jubilation radiated through his body as he took her hand in his and kissed it. "You've just made me the happiest man in the country."

"That was my intention." She lifted the wicker lid. "What did you pack?"

"All your favorites. Allow me." He added a piece of fried chicken and several slices of peaches onto her plate. Snatching a biscuit, he slathered it with orange marmalade. "Here you go."

"You're awfully sweet." She picked up a biscuit and savored a bite.

Her little moan of pleasure made him long to sample her mouth like he had last night. "I remember the delicious food at our church picnics."

"I used to help Ma bake sugar cookies. Rolling out the dough had been my favorite part, probably because I got to eat the scraps." A faraway look glimmered in her green eyes. One that might be longing, but he couldn't be certain.

"Your ma and mine used to swap recipes. Get those two together and they'd talk for hours about cooking." Nothing had been better than his mom's home-cooked meals. Ones he'd never taste again.

"We were all sad when your Ma died, and your family moved away." She bit her bottom lip. "And my ma joined her maker a year later."

"That must have been hard. I'm sorry." He needed to lighten the mood. "Enough with the sad times. Let's talk about the crazy things we did as kids. You already know about the outhouse escapade, so I figure it's your turn to share."

"No sirree. You started this so you go first."

"Fine. Remember how we used to play hide-and-seek in the hillside behind your shop?"

She nodded.

"Anyway, I hid behind a tree and stepped on something."

Her eyes widened. "What was it? Wait don't tell me. I bet you saw a skunk because I had been counting to ten and you came barreling by me stinking to high heaven."

"Talk about embarrassing. Plus, I smelled so bad my folks made me sleep in the barn."

She laughed for the longest time, and he couldn't resist joining in.

"Now it's your turn."

"I did a lot of silly things like catching frogs and chasing butterflies and ruining my new boots by stepping into mud puddles. Got the paddle for that one."

"Did that happen often?"

"Not for me. As you probably remember being the only girl, Pa adored me. He tended to be tougher on Jamey."

"Being the oldest comes with extra responsibilities." He knew that firsthand. If his younger brother hadn't married and started his own life, he'd still be looking out for him.

"Could you get me more cider?" she asked.

He refilled her glass.

"Tell me the truth. Are the streets of Sacramento made of gold like the stories suggest?" She gave him a playful push.

"Nope. It rains so much that the muddy ground is like walking on muck."

"You just ruined my fantasy of a perfect town." She snatched a piece of chicken.

"This town isn't bad. Not with you in it." He couldn't help staring at those expressive eyes. Now they bloomed with a hint of delight. "Besides being beautiful, I admire your strength. I don't know another gal who works in the family's blacksmith shop." His thumb drew a line along her chin, cupped her face with his palm and leaned forward to kiss her. Pulling back to take a breath, he whispered. "I wish I didn't have to leave you tomorrow."

"Me, too."

He pressed his forehead against hers. "I promise to come calling next weekend."

"I'm counting on it."

Once again, he brought his mouth to hers.

CHAPTER 11

As Chantilly made breakfast Monday morning, she couldn't stop thinking about how Blaze's kisses made her insides quiver.

"Hey, sis," her brother said from the table.

She startled.

"You're skittish this morning. What's gotten into you?"

As if she could admit to the surge of excitement funneling through her body. She straightened up taller, and said, "You surprised me, that's all." With a quick flick of her wrist, she salted the eggs. "Did you enjoy your time at the ranch?"

"Boy did I. Daniel, Bill, and I raced horses by the river, and I won. Can you believe it?"

She could believe Daniel lost on purpose to pick up Matt's spirits.

Her thoughts drifted to the dance and Daniel saying he'd like to court her. Four years older than her in school, he'd barely spoken to her. He didn't become Jamey's friend until a couple of years ago. He'd been nice enough, but that was it. Why'd he say something now? The whole notion just didn't make sense. Maybe he didn't feel right seeing as he had been so close with Jamey. Men could be difficult to understand.

"Then we watched cowboys breaking broncos. Daniel said I could try breaking one the next time I'm there. Figured I'd be a natural with all my know-how about horses." His words spilled so fast he hardly paused for a breath. "Someday he might let me tame Reckless."

"Reckless?" Her heart stopped. Experienced cowboys broke their necks on the backs of powerful horses with names like Reckless and Devil's Due.

"The bronc's big and mean. Daniel says the right man can make him rideable." Matt shoveled eggs into his mouth.

What was Daniel thinking? She counted to five and tried to sound calm. She wanted to give Daniel a piece of her mind for encouraging an inexperienced teen like Matt to try such a foolish thing.

"What about your studies and helping Flynn? I

thought you enjoyed working with animals and learning science."

"I do. But even if I could attend college, that would take years. If'n I work on a ranch, I'd get to wrangle calves and cattle. Maybe even help birth a few or fix up ones that get caught in barbed wire. And it'd be a lot more entertaining than forging metal." Matt dropped his fork, and it clanged on his plate.

"Is Daniel in town today?"

"Yep. Said he come by the shop early."

By the time she'd cleaned up the kitchen and walked out, she found Daniel waiting on a nearby bench at the side of the shop.

She strode over to him. "How dare you suggest Matt break horses? I can't lose him."

"Chant, calm down." He patted her hand.

"Not when you're suggesting someday Matt will be on Reckless." She clenched her fingernails into her hands.

"I never said that. The boy's smart about animals and knows more than I'll ever understand. Last month he showed me the books Flynn loaned him on doctoring. I simply told him that with his smarts and instincts about animals, I wouldn't be surprised to see him tame a beast like Reckless."

She let out a long breath. "You're right about him

being smart. He reads his books over and over and has memorized all the terms."

"Your brother should study medicine or maybe even become a doctor. Has he applied to a university yet?"

"If only we had the money." They weren't poor, but they couldn't afford the tuition, much less room and board for her brother.

He put his hand on her shoulder and gave her a sincere smile. "Don't fret. You know I'm here for you and Matt. I'd like to take you two out for dinner next time I'm in town."

"Maybe." She thought about mentioning that Blaze was courting her, but Daniel acted as a friend. She wasn't interested in Daniel as a man, but if he could help her brother, she'd be grateful.

CHAPTER 12

For the third time in two weeks, Matt came home late smelling like whiskey. Her stomach twisted in knots. Jamey hadn't started drinking until he turned sixteen not fourteen like Matt. Even then, he'd been able to hold his liquor.

About a year ago, Jamey started gambling. And now he's gone.

No way would Matt follow in his brother's footsteps. No way would she lose her only kin. Not when he had such a promising future.

What could she do to fix this?

The deed came to mind. Maybe she could talk Matt into selling the property. The only problem was that she doubted it would be worth much. Still, since she'd never taken the time to read the deed, she wanted to see exactly what it said. The last time she'd spotted the document, she believed it had been in one of the pigeonholes or cubbies inside the desk. Lighting a lamp, she rolled down the top.

She picked up a stack of papers and came across a newspaper clipping announcing the opening of the blacksmith shop in 1845. Memories of her family's happiness flooded her mind.

Footfalls came closer interrupting her thoughts. "What ya doing?" Based on the way Matt rubbed his eyes, she'd woken him up. Good because he'd woken her up when he tromped in the house around midnight.

"Looking for the deed."

"Why?" A frown tipped Matt's mouth.

"Since Jamey passed, we need to change it into your name." A niggling at the back of her mind said they should have done this right away.

"Okay." Her brother shrugged. "Can I help?"

"That'd be great." Even tired, her sweet, caring brother could still be thoughtful. "Why don't you start with the top drawer? I'll check the pigeonholes and cubbies."

Matt took out the contents, piled a stack of papers on the kitchen table, and plopped into a chair. He handed her an official-looking document with the Seal of Nevada imprinted at the top of the page. "Any idea if this has been paid?"

. . .

NEVADA PROPERTY TAX BILL. The amount of $90 is hereby due December 31, 1860.

"NOT SURE. Think you could stop by the courthouse and pay it."

"No problem, Sis. I'll take care of this after school." His shoulders slumped. "With Pa and Jamey gone things have gotten harder."

Which would explain his drinking. Her agitation toward her brother softened. He suffered the same as she.

In a bottom cubby, she pulled a rectangular parchment.

MAY 8, 1860. Bank of Comstock. Pay to Jamey Walsh.

"YOU WILL NOT BELIEVE THIS!"

"You found the deed." Matt's eyebrows lifted.

"Not exactly, but this is a draft for a hundred dollars." Excitement coursed through her.

"You're joshing."

"See for yourself." She handed him the draft as giddiness washed over her.

"Bet Jamey won this playing cards." His eyes lowered.

"I knew about his gambling. I didn't like it, but what he did with his portion had been his business."

"He taught me Faro. Sometimes he brought me along to the Silver Dollar." Matt puffed out his chest. "Once I turned five dollars into twenty."

"Matt, please stay out of the saloons."

Her brother grunted.

Again, she reminded herself that she wasn't his mom. At fourteen he was almost a man.

Matt held up a five by seven document. "I found the deed, but it says at the bottom, page one of two. I wonder what's on the second part." He handed the paper to her.

"I do not know. I suppose we'll have to keep on searching."

CHAPTER 13

Blaze arrived in town Friday evening. After settling in at Missy's Boarding House, he thought he might as well wet his whistle at the Golden Horse-shoe Saloon, so he headed across the street.

Inside, miners and cowboys leaned against the long mahogany bar. Blaze slipped into an empty spot near the end.

"What'll it be, sir?" The bartender's yellow teeth practically matched his shirt.

"Whiskey." Blaze looked at the painting of a scantily clad woman behind the bar.

"Four bits," the bartender said.

Charging fifty cents felt like getting hoodwinked, but Blaze retrieved the money from his pocket and paid.

The bartender handed him a glass. The watered-down whiskey had a bite of chili pepper. Not that he cared about getting sloshed, he just needed a little liquid refreshment.

"Got an empty spot for cards over here!" Jed waved from a table in the corner.

Cards sounded like an entertaining way to kill some time. He walked over. "What are you playing?"

"Twenty-one."

"I'm in." He sat in a chair.

"This here is Sparky. He works in the Blacksmith shop," Jed said.

"Nice to meet you." Chantilly had mentioned him a time or two. Blaze shook his hand.

The man on the far left who wore a Stetson glanced up but didn't say a word. Just put a dollar on the table.

Jed added a quarter as did Sparky, so Blaze did the same.

The dealer dealt each of them one card face up and left his down. With the second card, Blaze ended up with a king and an eight. Not bad but not enough to double the bet. He put his hand flat on the table indicating he'd stay.

When the dealer went over, he ended up winning.

"Must've brought luck with you," Jed said.

"Hope so."

A heavily painted brunette came over with a bottle

and shot glasses. "Can I interest you fellows in a drink?"

Blaze raised his hand. As she poured, she leaned over him and whispered in his ear. "Anything else I can do for you?"

"Just the whiskey." Chantilly was the woman he wanted. No doubt she snuggled in front of a fire reading a novel.

The dealer took the second round with an ace and a king. Blaze won the third with two jacks.

"Yippee!" somebody shouted, accompanied by loud cheers in a side room. With so many people standing around he couldn't see a thing.

Blaze threw in his hand. "I'm gonna check out the Faro game. It had never been his thing, but it could be interesting to watch.

He made it about several feet when a buxom blonde in a skimpy outfit displaying far too much cleavage put her arm around his shoulder.

"Hey, handsome. How 'bout I show you a good time?" Her red lips and coal-black eyelashes cheapened her youthful features.

"Not tonight."

He heard a skinny man in overalls ask the faro dealer, "I'm new to this. How do you play?"

"Players place bets on one of the thirteen cards," the dealer's deep voice called. "I'll turn over two cards. If your card is not drawn, the bet stays or can be moved for the next hand. If your wager is on the first card, you lose your bet. You win double whatever you put down if the wager is on the second."

"I'm in." The man threw down a dollar on ten, then others joined in.

"Buck the tiger," somebody shouted. At least a dozen men teemed around the table.

A lanky fellow put down a few coins and took a swig from a whisky bottle.

Blaze scrunched his eyes as he took a second look. Matt?

"We've got ourselves a winner," the dealer called.

He scanned the people next to Matt and immediately recognized Daniel urging him on as he clapped the boy on his shoulder.

Blaze had to weave through a few men to get closer. Matt scooped up coins from the table and shoved them into his pocket. The fact Matt won a handful of coins meant he must have bet a decent amount of money which he could have just as easily lost. He'd seen it before. The problem with winning is that men sometimes caught the gambling fever and ended up losing much more than their shirt.

Daniel pushed past Blaze and moved toward the swinging doors leaving Blaze to wonder why he left the boy.

Matt stood and stumbled toward the bar. "Another

whiskey."

The bartender slid a glass to him.

Blaze moved into an empty seat right next to the boy. "Hello, Matt."

"Blaze?" Matt turned. "What're you doing here?"

"Just got in town."

"You winning too?"

"Not exactly." After three hands he'd broke even.

Matt picked up his glass and swayed.

This kid's had a little too much to drink. I needed to get him home. Blaze placed an arm around the back of his shoulders and steadied the teen. "Come along."

"Let's go to the Red Dawg. Gonna win big there, too." Matt floundered forward as he tried to stand.

Blaze wrangled Matt's arm around his waist and led him outside. "Keep moving."

"Yes, sir. Got a pocket full of money to double. Could use another whiskey, too."

It seemed like fighting a wayward calf as he wrangled the teen to keep progressing forward along the boarded walkway, turned up the block to reach the blacksmith shop, and weaved behind to the cabin where he and Chantilly lived.

"That's my place." Matt put his finger over his mouth. "Shhhhh. Quiet. We don't want to wake Chantilly." He opened the door and knocked over a jar. It shattered with a thunderous clatter.

"What's going on?" Chantilly shrieked and ran into the parlor. With her long dark hair flowing down to her waist, he couldn't help but appreciate how gorgeous she appeared.

"We were having a little fun," Matt garbled.

She eyed Blaze from the doorway.

Matt held out a handful of silver dollars. "I won this at the Golden Horsssss-shoe."

"How much did you lose?"

"Nothing. I'm on a winning s-treak."

"You smell like Jamey did when he's been out drinking," she huffed. "And so do you Blaze."

He held up his hands. "I found your brother like this and brought him home."

"What were you doing in the saloon?" She gave him a dirty look.

"Playing a few hands of cards."

"You're just like Jamey. Hanging out in saloons and losing hard-earned money. I thought you were different." She put her hands on her hips and glared at Blaze.

"Woman, you don't have a clue what you're talking about."

"Really. I just buried my brother because someone shot him over a card game."

"I'm sorry, but that has nothing to do…"

She cut him off. "I'm tired and need to get Matt to bed. See yourself out."

"Tilly, we need to talk."

"Not tonight. Just go. Please." She pushed Matt toward his room.

"I'll be back tomorrow," Blaze called from the doorway.

He walked along the dirt alleyway. Chantilly wouldn't listen to him and acted like he coerced Matt into being his drinking pal.

He made it to the boarding house.

"How are you doing?" the owner asked.

"Well, thank you." He put on his best smile. "Think you could do some laundry for me."

"Of course. Ten cents a garment. Leave your things outside your door, and I'll have your clothing back tomorrow afternoon."

"Appreciate it."

"Anything else I can do for you?"

"That should be it." He headed up the stairs to his room and tugged off his boots.

Chantilly will understand once she thinks things through.

He pulled off his pants and shirt.

Can't blame her for protecting her brother.

He sifted through his clothing and kept his cleanest shirt and pants, before throwing the rest in a large basket and placing it outside the door. Stripped down to his long johns, he flopped onto the mattress.

Better get some shuteye.

CHAPTER 14

Blaze's mind filled with images of Chantilly flipping her long braid behind her. He unraveled her hair and ran his fingers through her silky tresses and leaned in to kiss her.

A rooster cock-a-doodle-dooed his morning greeting. He woke with a start, holding his hand against his racing heart.

Just a dang dream.

Songbirds chirped right outside his window.

"Be quiet! Let me sleep," he shouted. But none of the creatures paid him any mind. He put his pillow over his head to shut out the noise. That didn't help at all.

Might as well get up.

Sunlight shone through the open curtains. He looked out the boarding house window. A handful of people were out on the streets. Figuring it must be around seven, he might as well get breakfast.

He dressed and headed to the dining room. The aroma of eggs, bacon, potatoes, and flapjacks made his stomach growl, so he went to the side counter and filled his plate.

He sat at an empty spot next to a young family. The mother held a toddler in her lap and fed him. A fantasy of Chantilly holding their child made his heart ache for a family of his own.

An hour later he stood outside Chantilly's door rocking back and forth on his feet as his chest tightened and squeezed. He raised his fist and knocked.

The door creaked open a few inches. The smile she wore vanished the moment she saw him.

"Give me a minute of your time."

Her shoulders dropped, and she let out a little sigh. "Fine. Let's sit at that bench under the eucalyptus tree."

He stepped back but stayed near her as she closed the door. She scampered away from him to a secluded bench about fifty yards away.

"Good morning, Tilly." He moved in next to her.

She looked down.

"I can't allow you to court me anymore." She folded her arms across her chest.

"Why? Because I was in a saloon?"

"That's part of it. Were you gambling?"

"I sat in on a card game and had a few shots of whiskey." He looked at her furrowed brow, wondering why she got so upset. Most men enjoyed a game of cards on occasion.

"Jamey used to play cards and drink." She squinted at him.

"I'm not Jamey."

"I know that. But you guys were best friends at one time, and you still seem to have a lot in common with him." Her mouth quivered.

"That's not fair." He tried to grasp her hand, but she set it in her lap.

"It's how I see it."

He couldn't let that come to pass. "I helped your brother last night. Doesn't that count for anything?"

"Yes," she sighed. "It's just he's following in Jamey's footsteps. I can't lose him too."

"You won't."

"Don't you get it? When I went out with you, I lost sight of what is most important to me. My family. I must come up with a better solution for Matt."

"I can help with that."

"By hanging out in saloons? I don't think so. Besides, this is my problem, not yours."

Blaze stood, shaking his head. "I don't get it, Chantilly. I like you. Always have. I'm quite certain you like me." He paced in front of her. "Didn't our dinner or dance or picnic together mean anything to you? It did to me." Desperation crept into his voice.

"At the time I thought so, but now I realize I acted selfish." Her lips pressed together in a firm line. "We're through."

"You're wrong about me." He'd done nothing bad.

"None of this matters. I don't want to see you anymore."

"I'll be back in a week. Can I call on you then?"

"Blaze, it's over. Just accept my decision."

"I can't."

Feeling hollow inside, he strode away, all the while questioning how he had lost the girl who captured his heart.

CHANTILLY REMAINED on the bench fighting back tears. She breathed in frigid air, exhaling a wispy puff of white breath.

In and out.

Blaze's kisses might have made her toes tingle, but she couldn't risk a relationship with him. She needed security for both herself and Matt.

In and out.

She refused to be conned by another with pretty lies.

Footsteps scrunched on the ground behind her, and she looked over her shoulder expecting Blaze—not Daniel.

"Saw your fellow leaving." Sparkling blue eyes like the sky shone as he tipped his hat.

"Mind if I have a seat? I have something I'd like to talk with you about."

She gave a devil-may-care twist of her wrist. "Okay."

"You're shaking." Daniel took her hand in his.

"My brother went out drinking and gambling." And Blaze just happened to be at the same saloon. Coincidence or not. It didn't matter.

"From what I heard about him last night, he got tipsy." Daniel chuckled.

"I do not find Matt's drunken stupor funny." It was bad enough folks gossiped about Jamey, but now Matt would be fodder for the fire.

"It's really nothing to worry your little head over. He's just sowing wild oats."

"Tell me about your wild days. I've noticed how the women flock around you."

"Yeah, I've had my fun, but that doesn't mean I'm a bad man." He placed his hand on her shoulder. "You've had a rough go of it for the last few weeks. I'm here as your friend."

"I could use one. Sorry about the comment. It's just after Jamey's death I'm still a bit frazzled."

"Anything I can do to help?"

"Keep Matt out of the saloons. I'm afraid he'll end up like Jamey." He'd die and leave her all alone.

"Like I said before, he's a smart boy. He'd excel in college."

As if she had the money. "I wish I could send him."

"I'm here for both of you. I've got some connections and will see what I can do."

The last thing she wanted was to be beholden to Daniel. Still, if he could figure out a better future for her brother, she'd be more than willing to listen. "Thank you, Daniel."

"No problem. That's what friends do for each other." He squeezed her hand offering her a sense of security. "I'll be in town in a couple of days and will check on you."

"That would be nice."

"There's another reason I stopped by. I'm having a shindig at my place and could use a woman's touch. Think you'd be willing to help me host the party?"

"Absolutely." A party sounded grand. She found her spirits picked up substantially.

CHAPTER 15

Sunday morning, on his way to church, Blaze hoped if he prayed hard enough God would decide he was the right man for Chantilly. Waiting just past the general store, he spotted her walking with her brother and stepped next to her. "Morning, Tilly, Matt."

"Hey, Blaze." Matt nodded.

"Hello."

He glanced over at Chantilly. Her stiff posture and grim expression said she hadn't been happy to see him. "You look fetching this morning."

"Thank you." Her voice came out clipped.

"See anything exciting on your last route?" Matt asked as they continued walking.

"Other than a band of wild horses, it was a rather boring trip."

"But you get to ride like the wind. It's fun, right?"

"It's a job. I get up at the crack of dawn and ride till sundown. Weather can be a pain. And don't get me started on the last time my horse threw a shoe. Once I had to walk over a mile to reach town." He liked his job, but he thought of it as just a means to an end. "I think with your book smarts you could do something better."

"I suppose."

Blaze glanced over a Chantilly. Her lips quirked upward.

They reached the corner of the church.

Chantilly stopped him with her hand. "Blaze, I told you this is over," she said with a flat tone.

He wanted to argue but based on the glare she gave him, he kept quiet.

"Sorry." Matt shrugged as he looked at him.

"Let's go," she told her brother, and they headed toward the front of the building where she marched up the steps with Matt tailing behind her.

He could not move, yet everyone around him seemed to be in a hurry. Buggies parked. Horses were tied to hitching posts. People scurried into the church.

"You coming inside?" Jed asked.

Blaze hadn't even seen the man move next to him. "I-I reckon." A little help from the almighty would be appreciated.

"Are you okay?"

"Been better."

"Then you're at the right place. Can't tell you how many times I've gone inside, and my troubles vanished."

If only things were that easy. Still, he followed his friend into the white chapel, ambled up the aisle, and scooted into the last pew right behind Chantilly.

Blaze nodded at several people, townsfolk he used to know.

Matt turned around and looked at Blaze with a pained expression on his face.

Good. The boy should be sorry about his actions last night.

Matt whispered a little too loudly, "Blaze is sitting right behind you."

She stiffened and straightened her back.

The pastor shuffled to the pulpit. "Welcome, everyone. I'm glad all you folks joined us on this fine day." He pushed his round glasses up on his nose. "Praise the Lord."

"Praise the Lord," Blaze said with the rest of the congregation.

"Our first hymn is 'Glory to God.'"

The choir sang. Packed in close on the hard bench, he itched to reach over and fiddle with the ribbon in Chantilly's braid but resisted the temptation.

The preacher's topic turned out to be forgiveness

which worked for Blaze. He tried to catch her eye, while she stared at the front.

"Just like God has forgiven our sins, we must forgive others." It seemed as if the man of the cloth heard his pleas. "Love thy neighbor."

Chantilly squirmed, leaned back, and glared at him.

He scooted forward and whispered in her ear, "Forgive me." Except for playing cards and having a couple of drinks, he had done nothing wrong. But he hoped asking for forgiveness might help ease her angst.

"I have. I just can't be with you," she said through clenched teeth.

"Are you having trouble with the little lassie?" Jed asked quietly.

"Yep."

"That's too bad." Jed stood and picked up his hymnal as did the rest of the congregation.

They sang, "All Things Bright and Beautiful."

The song should be uplifting with words about how everything in the world has beauty. Unfortunately, without Chantilly at his side the world seemed drab.

A few more hymns were sung, and the service ended.

Being in the last pew, he filed toward the foyer exit, greeted the pastor, and walked down the steps to wait for Chantilly at the side.

Matt came out first and headed toward a group of teens. Chantilly rushed past him.

Blaze had to run to catch up to her. "Have lunch with me. Talk this out," he spoke in her ear.

"That's not a good idea. As I told you yesterday, I can't allow you to court me any longer."

He reached for her arm. "Please don't give up on us."

"Let it go, Blaze." She pulled away from him and dashed along the boarded walkway.

He just stood there staring as the words sunk in. It was really over.

CHAPTER 16

Snow capped the distant Sierra Nevada Mountains as Blaze did his Monday route. Normally, he appreciated the majestic beauty. The wide-open range with only a scattering of cabins made him feel free and happy. But today trouble filled his soul.

The weekend started out hopeful. Getting in on Friday night, he had planned to use Saturday to get spiffied up for his date with Chantilly. Maybe stop by the confectionery to buy her something sweet. Too bad the weekend ended in heartbreak.

He reached Miller's Landing, exchanged his mochila, and took off again. In the distance, a herd of deer grazed on sagebrush. A long-eared jack hopped along the trail, and he kept on riding fast.

He thought back to Friday night at the saloon.

Discovering Matt hanging out in a bar. Not unusual or illegal by any means. Still, it seemed odd he didn't drink with any friends his age. The only one he recognized standing next to him had been Daniel. Daniel, who was supposedly a friend to the family.

Blaze didn't trust the guy. Even as a kid, Daniel had bullied people to bend to his will. Older than him and Jamey, he and his two friends would pick on younger kids or tease little girls and make them cry, or even steal lunches. Several times, he'd corner Jamey and him on their way home and push them around. One time, the two of them fought back which resulted in a black eye for Jamey and a broken rib for himself. Daniel and his goons knew how to bully, threatening if either of them told they get them worse the next time.

It stunned him that Jamey became friends with this creep. Still, people could change.

Although he seriously doubted Daniel had. In fact, he wouldn't be surprised if Daniel was up to something.

What if Chantilly put all her faith in him? From what she'd said she seemed to think him a good friend.

It irritated him that Chantilly had pushed him away. She should be grateful. After all, he managed to get Matt out of the saloon and safely home. But she seemed to focus on the fact that he drank and played cards. How in Hades would he get Chantilly to see he had nothing to do with her brother's escapades? He wanted to make her realize how much he'd loved her his entire life.

Then he thought about how Jamey's death played a number on her mind. The resentment she harbored for his abandonment might never go away.

He kept on riding, exchanging mailbags at various stops. The whole time his mind whirled with frustration.

He had plans, plans that included making enough money to buy a ranch. And settling down and starting a family. He desired Chantilly to be a part of his plans.

He made it to his last stop for the night, Cold Springs, rode toward the stables just inside the walls and hung his mochilla on the hook. "Hey, Jack," he dismounted and handed over his horse.

"Catch any snow this trip?"

"Not so much as a flake." The whole route had been pretty uneventful.

"Good to hear."

"Think the weather will stick," Blaze asked.

Jack wet his finger and put it in the air. "Maybe for another day or two."

People had odd ways of predicting weather, but he said nothing about it. "I'd better get going. Hopefully, I can still nab a hot bowl of stew."

"I'd try Goldie's. It's the best in town and only a block south of here."

"That's where I'll head. See you at the crack of dawn."

Being Monday, only a scattering of people lined the streets, mostly miners and cowboys. Striding on the boarded walkway, he glimpsed at the shop signs, walked past a vacant lot, and headed inside Goldie's Restaurant and Saloon. A skinny man with his arm in a sling sat at the only empty table.

"Mind if I join you?"

"Not at all."

"Name's Blaze."

"Zeke." He offered his hand.

As they shook, he stared at the man's face. He figured life hadn't been kind to the fellow lately. A part of him wanted to ask what had transpired but the other part said to leave things alone.

A busty cocktail waitress sauntered up. "What can I get you fellows?" Her eyes remained glued to Blaze's as she gave a little shimmy.

"I'm starving. You got anything left in the kitchen?" His stomach grumbled.

"Chicken stew."

"I'll take a bowl and coffee to go with that?"

"Whiskey's cheaper." She winked.

"No thanks."

"And you?"

Zeke ordered a beer.

The saloon girl walked away adding an extra sway in her hips.

"You new around here?" Zeke asked.

"Somewhat. I'm a Pony Express rider and have been doing this route for a little over a month."

"Well, I'll be. Ain't never met a rider before. Heard you've got to dodge arrows along with bad weather."

"No arrows, but this winter's been pretty cold."

The saloon girl brought out the drinks with his soup and a plate of buttered bread. "When you're done with that, I'll be more 'n happy to sate any other appetites."

"Not tonight, darling." He picked up his spoon and shoveled in the stew. It might not be the tastiest food he'd ever had, but it turned out to be warm and filling.

CHAPTER 17

Tuesday morning, Chantilly sat outside and appreciated the sunny and rather warm day for January.

"Penny for your thoughts," Daniel asked as he walked up.

"Um, I'm just enjoying the weather."

"It is rather nice." He motioned to the bench. "Mind if I join you?"

"Not at all."

"Matt told me about your breakup with Blaze." He reached for her hand.

She pulled away, unsure of what he wanted.

"Are you okay?"

"I am. I'd rather talk about your upcoming party, though."

"Fine with me. How 'bout we take a stroll to the bakery? I'll buy you a cinnamon roll and we can iron out the details."

"All right." It'd been weeks since she last visited the establishment and her mouth watered thinking about the sweet rolls.

He offered his arm. They walked along the dirt trail and up to the boardwalk. She glanced at Daniel. Her head reached the bottom of his shoulders—with Blaze it met his chin. Daniel's light hair—a contrast to Blaze's dark wavy locks.

She told herself to quit thinking about Blaze. Their relationship was over.

"You look pretty this morning?"

Not hardly. She had pulled her hair into a high ponytail. Plus, she wore her least favorite dress. The peach floral.

A couple of men milled in front of the general store. They continued another block and then went inside the bakery. Cakes, breads, and sweet rolls were displayed on a long counter with three shelves above. The baker wrapped an item in paper for an older couple. The couple walked out hand in hand. Watching them, she realized she would never have a future like that with Blaze. A future where she'd have someone she could always lean on.

Daniel led them to the table closest to the door and pulled out her chair.

The owner wiped her hands on her apron. "Hello, Chantilly. Daniel. What can I get you?"

"Two cinnamon rolls." He turned to Chantilly. "You want coffee?"

"Yes, please." Given her melancholy mood this morning, she appreciated having someone else take control for a change.

She cut her roll and bit into a yummy morsel. The yeasty cinnamon concoction combined with sugary icing sang "Alleluia" in her mouth. "This is delicious."

"I wholeheartedly agree." He gave a mischievous wink. "About the party, I'll be holding the event in the old barn, like my folks used to do before they passed. It's solid but hasn't been used for much lately."

He'd lost both his folks several years back during a fluke stagecoach accident.

"That sounds lovely. Who have you invited?"

"All of the local business owners, farmers, neighbors and quite a few of the townsfolk. Figure there will be well over a hundred in attendance."

"That's quite a crowd."

"The more the merrier." He sat up straighter.

"Do you have plenty of tables and chairs? I know most folks will dance, but it would be nice to offer a place to sit."

"We should have plenty. Have you ever been to my place?"

"No." Townsfolk often gossiped about how nice things were inside Daniel's grand house. "I've ridden past."

"Then you'll be in for a treat when you come to the party. I'll be in town this Saturday. How about I take you to dinner?" Daniel raised a brow.

"All right." Dinner would be nice. Plus, maybe he could help her figure out a way to get Matt out of the saloons.

"Terrific. Saturday around six." He took her hand to his mouth and kissed it. "I've got more than the party to discuss with you."

What else could he want? He'd already expressed his interest in her so it couldn't be that. No reason to stress. Whatever he said couldn't be worse than suffering with her brother's death.

An hour later, she worked on shoes for the banker's horse. Using her tools to create something useful out of metal made her happy. Too bad what she did wouldn't be enough to pay for Matt's tuition.

As she picked up the front hoof and nailed in a shoe, Jed walked up.

"Hey, you." She set down the foot. "How are things?"

"Busy as usual." He passed her a letter. "Blaze said to give you this."

"Thanks."

"You have a good day." Jed strolled off whistling "Oh Susanna."

She stood there for several seconds staring at the note. A part of her said to ignore it but her curiosity won. Opening the envelope, a lacy, off-white ribbon flittered out. She caught it, holding it in her hand as she unfolded the letter.

DEAR TILLY,

The lacy ribbon makes me think of you. Beautiful. Intriguing. Full of life.

I love how your eyes light up when you are enthralled. I love your stubbornness and tenacious strength. I love you.

Please give me another chance.

Loving regards,

Blaze

BLAZE HAD the nerve to say he loved her. Didn't he get love was not important? Her family was important. She couldn't have Matt make the same choices as Jamey.

Fingering the delicate rose pattern in the lace, frustration had her pacing back and forth. How dare he try to win her over with a simple gift? The fact that he got her something she liked should please her, but it didn't.

It just made her agitated. She told them they were through. Why couldn't he leave her alone?

Pushing the note and ribbon back inside the envelope, she shoved it into her skirt pocket and stomped inside the blacksmith shop.

Sparky stopped hammering and smirked at her. "Saw Jed give you a letter, and I'm assuming it's from your fellow. I like Blaze."

"We're not together anymore."

"Oh," his brow rose. "Wanna talk about it."

"There's nothing to say." The notion that Blaze would encourage Matt to follow in her older brother's footsteps proved he wasn't the man for her.

"I can be a good listener." He gave her a one-armed hug.

She shook her head.

"If you ever change your mind, the offer's always open."

She stepped back, surprised at how much she needed that hug. The older man kind of reminded her of her pa. Genuine, hardworking, and strong.

CHAPTER 18

The next Saturday, Daniel brought Chantilly to the Warm Springs Hotel. Memories of the last time she visited there flooded her mind. Walking through the lobby on Daniel's arm, her heart failed to flutter like it had with Blaze. She chastised herself for thinking of him.

"Hello, Mr. Braddock," a hostess said to Daniel. "If you'll follow me, I'll show you to your table."

They were led past at least a dozen tables covered with white linen. Candles sparkled from the crystals on the massive chandeliers. He pulled out a chair for Chantilly at the same table where she shared supper with Blaze. She gazed at a landscape painting on the wall and thought about Blaze riding through hills similar to these as he delivered the mail.

"Your waiting staff should be with you shortly."

"I've ordered for us already." Daniel dismissed the hostess.

Chantilly unfolded the cloth napkin and set it on her lap.

A waitress approached their table and presented the label on a bottle of wine to Daniel.

"Perfect," Daniel said.

She opened the bottle and poured a sample into his glass.

He swirled the wine, tasted it, and nodded.

The woman poured red wine into his glass then hers.

"Napa Valley wines are excellent. To us and our party." He held up his glass and clinked it with hers.

Not bothering to correct him, after all it was *his* party, she took a sip and found the red wine bitter.

"I'll be right back with your soup," the server said.

"You look stunning tonight." Daniel smiled at her.

She figured she looked presentable in her Sunday best, a floral dress with a square collar but nothing out of the ordinary. "Thank you." He looked handsome in his pinstriped suit that accented his blue eyes, but he couldn't compare to Blaze. If only she could forget about him.

The young server brought out a basket of bread and two steaming bowls of French onion soup.

Eating a spoonful of the thick soup, she appreciated the cheesy flavor. "This is quite tasty." Taking a slice of bread from a checkerboard covered basket, she slathered it with butter.

"I assumed you'd like it." He finished his wine and poured more into each glass.

She took a sip of her water.

"How was your week?"

"Nice." Her days were peaceful.

He took out a folded sheet of paper from inside his suit jacket. "Here's the menu for our party. Of course, plenty of folks will bring desserts and side dishes."

It's *your* party, she wanted to say but now wasn't the time to be disagreeable, so she glanced at the food. Smoked ham, bacon, steak, and veal cutlets. Spinach and coleslaw salads. Orange slices. "Sounds delicious. I had no idea oranges grew in the winter."

"They do in California. Some parts never see a speck of snow."

Which proved to her how little of this world she had seen.

"What's Matt up to this evening?"

"He's out with friends."

"Matt's lucky to assist Flynn. The man's saved plenty of animals on my ranch."

"Matt loves trailing after him."

The server cleared their dishes.

Two plates with veal cutlets, green beans, and potatoes with a rich white sauce were set in front of them. Veal when she would have rather had stew. Daniel had chosen everything for their meal. She wished he had asked what she liked.

"Well, I've been mulling over Matt's gift with animals. Recently, I've read of a university in Pennsylvania that is offering animal science classes as electives. They're even considering offering a veterinarian program in the future. It sounds perfect for him." Determination filled his eyes. "There's an old friend of the family running the program, so I'm sure he'd been willing to help. I'd consider funding his endeavor if that works for both of you."

"Isn't there anywhere closer? Pennsylvania is a long way from here. I assumed there might be a college in San Francisco and no farther than the Midwest." Keeping Matt in Carson City when he had a world of opportunities waiting for him made her feel like a selfish person. Still, sending him away she'd be all alone, and she'd miss her brother's constant chatter and upbeat attitude.

"Not like this one."

"Oh."

"If Matt remains here, his opportunities are limited. As a farrier, he's wasting his talents." His voice got low. "He told me, man to man, that he finds the work rather tedious and hates how hot and confining the black-smith's shop gets in the summer."

She sucked in her breath because she loved the shop Pa build down to her core. But she couldn't expect her brother to feel the same way.

"I shouldn't have told you since Matt confided in me."

"I'm glad you did. You're just being honest." How else would she know Matt's wishes? She knew he loved her, but he also didn't want to hurt her feelings. Not after all they'd been through the last few years.

"What you and Matt do are your own concern," Daniel said in earnest.

"It's nice to have you as our friend."

"Always. Just like you, I want to see Matt better himself. It'd be good for him to get away from temptations of the saloons and gambling here." Daniel placed his hand over hers. "

He was right. Her brother deserved a better life.

"Of course, I'd expect him to pay me back at some point and would ask to hold the deed to your place as collateral."

"Why hold the deed? I don't get it." The place wasn't worth much.

"It's about forcing Matt to act like a man. If I give him the money, he might not take his studies as seriously."

Which was totally reasonable.

"If you hold the deed, would I still get to stay in the house?" She needed a place to live along with the profits.

"Where you live would be up to you."

As if she had any other choices.

"To be totally honest, I'm not just interested in Matt's welfare. I'm interested in you and would like us to be more than friends. As I said before, I want to court you."

Her mouth got dry. She swallowed hard.

His eyes shifted back and forth. "There's no reason to hold back my intentions. As we both know, life can be cut short."

The whole idea of a relationship with Daniel seemed too fast. Especially after the debacle with Blaze.

Could she allow Daniel to court her? Maybe. After all, he could help her brother which was all that really mattered.

CHAPTER 19

The next Saturday, Chantilly looked at herself in the mirror. Her new red dress might not be her first color of choice, but given she'd waited until yesterday to find one, she couldn't complain because it fit well.

This party should be fun. Too bad Daniel mentioned again that he wanted to court her. A little over a week ago, Blaze had been the one courting her. She had liked the easy banter they had with each other. Liked dancing with him. Who was she kidding? She liked kissing him.

Forget Blaze she told her crazy mind. Daniel could offer stability for her and Matt.

She brushed her hair a hundred times, something her ma taught her as a little girl, then braided it and wound it into a bun.

A rattling clamored outside.

Matt came out from his bedroom and rushed to the window. "You've gotta see this. Daniel hitched the buggy with his two best thoroughbreds, Thunder and Lightning." He swung the door open and didn't bother to close it as he dashed outside.

Daniel took the open door as permission to saunter in. Dressed to the teeth in a dark suit and white Stetson, he handed her a peppermint stick.

"How thoughtful." She laid the candy on the long thin table near the door.

"I'd have brought flowers but couldn't find any this winter."

"Candy's way better than stinking flowers." Coming back inside, Matt reached for the sweet stick, shoving the end into his mouth.

Daniel helped Chantilly into her hooded coat. She pulled the door closed and snaked her arm through his.

Matt sat in the driver's seat puffed up like a proud peacock.

Daniel helped her into the back seat then hopped in on the right, so close she sniffed pipe tobacco. She never cared for the smell.

"Thanks for coming early and agreeing to be a hostess."

She was there to make sure everything went smoothly.

"Hang on," Matt warned as he flicked the reins.

The horses lurched forward. They plodded along past the Red Dawn, Golden Horseshoe, and Carson Bonanza saloons. When they got to the Silver Dollar Saloon, she shut her eyes and tried to blot out Jamey's murder.

"We all miss Jamey," Daniel crooned as he placed his arm around the back of the seat.

"He died too young."

"He sure did. Every time I come to town, I expect to see him wearing a grin and ready to tell me the latest joke he'd overheard." Daniel tugged her closer.

"He had hundreds of 'em," Matt interjected. "What's the difference between a tube and a foolish Dutchman?"

She'd heard this one before. "One is a hollow cylinder and the other a silly Hollander."

The three of them chuckled.

"Here's one of my favorites." Daniel sat up taller. " What is a woman's favorite word?"

"Hmm… maybe a dress or bonnet?" That's something she would appreciate.

"No silly. The last one," Matt said.

While Matt and Daniel guffawed, she didn't find the joke at all funny. She gazed at the endless tundra covered in a layer of white and thanked the stars no snow was expected in the foreseeable future. In the distance a two-story house silhouetted to the north.

"Why is a dog like a tree?" Matt asked.

"Because they both lose their bark once they're dead," Daniel bantered.

Chantilly gasped. His reply hit deep in her soul. Life and death were far too easily interchanged.

"We're almost to the Double-B." Daniel said as they pulled under a wooden archway.

Hundreds of cattle ran free in the open fields. They passed an enormous stable bigger than a town's square. As they got closer to the house, it reminded her of an etching she'd seen in a newspaper featuring some ritzy mansion in the east. Or maybe a castle on a hillside in the middle of the desert.

Someday, she'd love to paint a landscape of this view.

The buggy stopped in front of the house, which was white with marble pillars adorning the porch. Not porch. *Veranda.*

Daniel helped her down. "Matt, park the carriage by the stables."

"Would you mind if I checked on Scarlet? I brought my doctoring book with me and would like to check to see how her leg is healing."

"Have at it." Daniel offered his arm. "That boy's full of curiosity."

"I think he might prefer animals to people." Even at a

young age, she'd catch him coddling a kitten in the barn or giving a horse a carrot instead of mucking out stalls. She turned and watched Matt flick the reins and drive away.

"Nothing wrong with that. Animals don't talk back," he said with a wink. "Let's go inside the house and I'll show you around."

Daniel escorted her up the wide staircase and inside the entryway. She tried not to gawk, but goodness, his formal living room had to be at least ten times larger than her cabin. The massive brick fireplace with a marble mantle commanded the room. Portraits and landscaped paintings adorned the walls. Fancy throw rugs covered the polished wood flooring. It reminded her of the rooms described in Jane Austen's novels. "Your house is beautiful."

"I'm glad you like it." He took her hand in his and brought her to a polished mahogany table so shiny she could see a blurred reflection of her face. He pulled out the first chair on the right side, waited for her to be seated, and took the head position. "Cookie will be right out with some refreshments."

A round woman with warm chestnut-colored eyes came out with a tray. "Cookie, this is Miss Walsh. She'll be helping with the party and has my permission to make any changes."

"Yes sir."

"Nice to meet you, miss. Would you care for coffee, tea, or hot chocolate?"

"Coffee, please."

"Same here. And I'd like you to bring out samples of a few of the items we'll be serving today."

"Yes, sir."

A few minutes later, Cookie brought out their drinks and their samples.

"That will be all for now." He excused the cook.

Chantilly sipped her coffee and sighed. The real cream was a treat from her usual milk. Then she took a bite of a roll filled with jam and whipping cream. "This is superb." For a moment she wondered what it would be like living here. Hosting parties. Spending her days with leisurely activities like knitting and embroidering. She got a little misty-eyed thinking of how her Ma considered her "all thumbs" when it came to doing delicate work.

"Try the green beans with bacon and carnalized onions. Next to veal, it's one of my favorites."

She savored a bite. "This is delicious."

"I had a feeling you'd be pleased. I've had three steers and a hog slaughtered, so we should have more than enough food with folks bringing their own specialties."

"That's quite generous of you."

"It's my pleasure." Daniel placed his hand on the back of her chair.

She nibbled on a slice of smoked beef and sighed. Daniel sure knew how to entertain with the right food.

"I'm looking forward to dancing with you."

His hint didn't go unnoticed. He wanted to court her.

Would that really be so bad?

CHAPTER 20

Chantilly spent the last two hours supervising the staff and cowboys on where to place things and doing various tasks. Now she stood at the barn entrance impressed with the transformation. Over a dozen linen cloths covered tables that were spread out at the right side. Delicate, silver oil lamps acted as centerpieces. Polished wooden floors left the center open for dancing and milling around.

A fiddler warmed up on a platform near the back. She recognized the musician as one of the cowboys who worked on the ranch. The drummer hit several rhythmic beats, while a cowboy strummed "Old Susanna."

Daniel moved beside her. "What do you think?"

"It's wonderful."

"You sure are. Come on." He took her hand and led her to the center of the floor. "May I have this dance?"

"There's no music."

He turned to the band. "Gentlemen, think you could play us a waltz?"

"Sure thing, boss," the fiddler said.

Daniel pulled her into his arms, and they were gliding across the floor. She let out a giggle when he spun her.

"Are you having fun?" he asked.

"I am."

The song ended and he let her go. "That's just a glimpse of what's ahead tonight."

A wagon clattered outside announcing the first guest.

He offered his arm. "Time for us to greet the folks."

It wasn't her party, still she put on her best smile.

A young couple with two kids in tow walked up. Occasionally, she'd seen them in town but never officially met them.

Daniel shook the man's hand. "Jack Simmons, Matty, I'd like to introduce you to Chantilly Walsh. Her brother owns the blacksmith shop in Carson City."

The comment irked her. Her brother might technically own it, but she and Sparky were the ones keeping it afloat.

"Nice to meet you," she nodded.

"Jack recently purchased the Smith's ranch."

Located closer to Genoa than to Carson, the ranch had remained vacant for ten years. She wondered if the man knew the last owner could never make a go of the land because his crops failed. He killed his wife before turning the gun on himself. Supposedly, the place was haunted.

But then again, that had been mere speculation.

"Where should I put these?" The woman held a platter of cookies.

"First table to your left."

A little girl pulled on the wife's skirt. "Ma, I'm thirsty."

"Bowls of punch and lemonade, along with decanters of hot cocoa and coffee, are right past the sweets." Chantilly motioned to the tables.

"If you're hungry for beef or smoked ham you'll find that on the long table," Daniel added. "Help yourself. The band will start up around two."

"Thank you," Jack said and walked away with his family.

"I'm gonna make sure my men are directing folks where to park," Daniel said and left.

More folks walked inside. She greeted the banker, assayer, and several families from town. Then the general store owner's wife moved next to her. "It's nice to be celebrating for a change."

"It sure is."

"Will Blaze be joining us later?" the husband asked.

"I don't believe so," she answered. While she had no idea what he might be up to, she hoped he wouldn't show.

Sparky escorted one of the miner's daughters, Pricilla. He'd been sweet on her ever since she arrived in town and judging by the way she shyly glanced up at him she felt the same.

There must have been close to a hundred guests milling around when the band announced the "Virginia Reel."

Daniel walked up, "May I have this dance?"

"Of course." The music played, and she found herself smiling as she wound her way through the circle, do-si-do-ing with Sparky, then clasping hands with Jed and Daniel. She ended up standing next to the banker when the song finished.

"Would you do me the honor of the next dance?" the banker asked.

"Sure." The number was a two-step. The man accidentally stomped on her toe at least three times before the song ended.

The band took a break.

Her grumbling stomach reminded her she had eaten little. She grabbed a plate, her mouth watered at the thought of sampling another one of those rolls filled with jam and whipped cream, but found the serving plate empty. Darn. She might as well try some smoked beef and potato salad.

"Looks like we're thinking alike."

She turned to see Sparky and asked, "Are you enjoying yourself."

"Yep. Promised Pricilla I'd get her food. Why don't you join us?"

"That sounds good." She followed Sparky to a table where the only empty spot had been right next to the preacher's wife and the schoolmarm.

"How are you doing, dearie?" the preacher's wife asked. Based on the way the woman's eyes narrowed as she frowned, she referred to Jamey's death.

Chantilly didn't want to think about her brother's demise tonight. She just wanted to have a good time, so she answered, "Well, thank you."

"That's wonderful," the woman said.

Chantilly turned to the teacher. "How is Matt doing in class?"

"Excelling as usual. He seems to devour every science book I find. To be honest, he is ready for something more challenging."

Which reminded her of Daniel's offer to help Matt in exchange for the deed. Her brother deserved so much more than this town could offer him.

After finishing her plate, she excused herself to get some fresh air outside.

Jed stood near a hitching post puffing on a stogie and talking with a group of cowboys. He waved at her. She waved back, but seeing she was the only female opted to go back in.

The band started up again. She ended up dancing countless rounds and several waltzes. Every now and then she'd look around for Blaze expecting to see him here since he should be off on Saturday. But he never showed. Probably for the better. She didn't need any reminders of what had been. She'd made the right decision calling things off.

Needing to sit for a spell, she headed over to some chairs near the back of the room.

"My, oh my. Chantilly sure is fickle," Doreen Richards from grade school said in a snippy tone. "One minute she's all doe-eyed over Blaze Steele, the next she's hanging on to every word Daniel says."

"I heard she just led Blaze on to make Daniel jealous," Abbigail O'Reilly added. "If you ask me, she's just a gold digger looking for a better life."

"Well, if she's setting her cap for Daniel, she's wasting her time," Doreen said. "If I couldn't get him interested in me, no way would he'd pick a drab little blacksmith's daughter."

"Hello." Chantilly stepped up to them. "I hope you're

having a good time." She'd grown up with their snide comments and learned long ago what they said didn't matter. Still, she did like making them squirm.

"We are," the women said in unison as their faces tinged with red.

"Good to hear." Daniel walked up and placed his arm around her shoulder. "If you'll excuse me, ladies, I'd like to dance with my girl."

The two were masters at agitating Chantilly and she'd been relieved when he whisked her away.

"Were they upsetting you?"

"Of course not." She let out a long sigh. Those women had always been malicious but there was no reason to let Daniel know they unsettled her.

She danced one more waltz. The party ended at around seven, giving folks plenty of time to get rested up for church the next day.

"You were a natural tonight." Daniel walked her to Jed's buggy. Her friend had promised to take her and Matt home.

"Thank you. This night turned out great."

"It did. How about dinner next Saturday?" he whispered in her ear.

"That should be fine." She still had things to discuss with him about Matt.

He kissed her cheek right in front of several townsfolk getting on horses or into buggies or wagons. And she tried not to cringe as she thought about Doreen and Abbigail calling her fickle.

Then he opened the door and helped her up inside the buggy.

"Daniel's sweet on you." Matt's grin widened as he sat next to her in the back seat.

"He's just a friend." A friend who cared about her and Matt.

CHAPTER 21

The following Saturday, Chantilly held Daniel's arm as they walked inside the El Dorado Restaurant and Inn located in the neighboring town. Snow flurried in the sky, and she wished they had just gone to the Warm Springs Hotel like before, but Daniel insisted the food was better here.

Adjusting the skirt of her blue taffeta gown, she followed him on floors so shiny they gleamed. They passed several round tables with white linen tablecloths and red cloth napkins folded into fancy fans. Candlelight shone from chandeliers in rainbow swirls.

She compared the opulent and swanky room with the Warm Springs Hotel. Considered fancy, in reality, the establishment was only a bit upscale from the local café.

The hostess seated at a table in the corner. She admired how his custom-made suit accented his wide shoulders.

"Give us your best bottle of champagne." Daniel winked at Chantilly.

The gesture made her squirm and not in a good way.

The server opened the champagne and poured it into two fluted glasses. Daniel picked up his glass. "To a special evening."

She clinked with him.

"Are you ready to order?" the server asked.

"Yes, we are. The lady and I will have prime rib."

Again, he chose for her without asking her preference. Maybe this shouldn't bother her, but it did. She refused to compare him to Blaze who seemed to respect her opinions. The two of them were over.

The server scurried off.

"Did you do anything entertaining this week?" Daniel asked.

"I helped fix an axel."

He eyed her sideways like she had gone crazy.

In Daniel's world, women should remain prim and proper and never get grease underneath their fingernails. Still, she had been proud of her accomplishment. She was about to speak when the food arrived.

So, she ate. The prime rib was tasty, although if she had her druthers, she would have chosen duck.

"I hope you're enjoying your meal." Daniel gave her a wide grin.

"I am."

"You know, a pretty woman like you shouldn't have to carry such a load on your shoulders. You should be able to enjoy your days and have the finer things in life."

"I really don't need much." She took a bite of potato and savored the rich creamy sauce.

"Alas, you deserve to be adorned in fancy gowns and fine jewelry."

Now and then, what woman didn't like a new dress or bobble? But her clothes were more than adequate. Her whole life had been tied to blacksmithing. She loved the hiss when horseshoes dropped in the water or the smell of forging hot metal.

"I'm enamored with you. You're not only beautiful, but intelligent and hardworking."

Why did her heart seem to stop with a thud? She put down her fork and stared at him.

He got down on one knee holding a small black box and took her right hand in his. "This may seem sudden, but as we both have realized, life can be short. I need a good woman to share my life. And I'd like you to be the one. Marry me."

"M-marry you?" Uncertainty shot through her

veins. Marriage would be a lifelong commitment. She should feel honored Daniel wanted her as a wife. After all, many of the girls in town had set their cap for him only to be let down.

His blue eyes twinkled. "You will have everything you could ever want. A big house. The most stylish clothes. Money to lavish on any whim you might have." He squeezed her fingers.

She bit her bottom lip.

"You know, Matt's already given his blessing to our union," he said in such a soft voice it tickled her ear.

He'd asked for her brother's permission, and she appreciated the thoughtfulness, but didn't like being rushed for a decision.

"You work too hard. Marry me and all that will change."

With Daniel, she'd have the perfect life. She'd have time to do things like riding in the hills, reading to her heart's desire, sleeping in late, and living a life of leisure.

He clasped her hand tightly, almost too tightly.

She felt like a rabbit with its foot caught in a trap. "There are a great deal of changes for me to consider."

"I don't mean to push, Chant." His eyes caught hers, and she looked down. "It's just I can't wait for us to start our life together."

Why didn't she simply say yes? Daniel would be a good provider.

He stood and leaned over and pressed his mouth against hers.

She waited for her heart to flutter, for a quiver deep inside, for tingling excitement to course through her body.

Nothing.

Still, his kiss was pleasant and acceptable. Certainly not repulsive.

People clapped. Obviously to them, their kiss meant the deal had been sealed.

"Let me think on it." She attempted to pull her hand away, but he held firm.

"In three weeks, it'll be Valentine's Day." Daniel slid his ring onto her finger. "I can't wait to turn my sweet valentine into my blushing bride."

"But I didn't say yes."

"You will. It's the best thing you can do for both you and your brother." He brought her hand to his mouth. "We'll have a great life together."

She wanted to scream *You're not listening to me! I didn't accept your proposal!* Yet, the rational side said he had a point. Matt could go downhill fast if she didn't get him out of this town.

And if she were really lucky, she'd get her happily

ever after with Daniel. Her own prince riding up on a white steed to save the day.

Except when she closed her eyes, an uninvited image of Blaze barged into her mind. She blinked several times to stop the craziness.

Blaze didn't get into town until late Saturday evening; thus, he didn't get to see Chantilly. He would chance sitting with her in Church on Sunday morning. Waiting near the hitching post, he saw the general store owners.

"Are you waiting for Chantilly?" the wife asked.

"As a matter of fact, yes."

"Oh dear," she flustered. "I know you're sweet on her, but ..."

"Myrtle," her husband said. "Leave him be."

"He deserves to know that Daniel and Chantilly are engaged."

Engaged. To Daniel.

"You don't know for certain." The husband clenched his teeth.

"I heard it from Josephine Jones who's visiting her daughter in Genoa. Anyway, they were dining in the El Dorado Restaurant, and she saw Daniel get down on one knee and slip a ring on her finger," the wife tutted.

His whole world seemed to go silent as he stared at nothingness. A crow cawed as it flew over his head, knocking him out of his daze.

Maybe the woman had been wrong. Several folks passed him, either scowling at him or giving him sorrowful looks.

He had to see for himself, so he started walking. A few feet ahead he spotted Chantilly clutching Daniel's arm as they walked up the stairs. A heaviness filled his heart as he fought off his disappointment. She should be with him.

Matt practically bounced behind them. He appeared happy. Blaze shouldn't wish the boy ill will but honestly, if Matt hadn't been in the saloon that day, this whole situation would be different.

Except he shouldn't blame everything on Matt. Obviously, Chantilly didn't feel as strongly as he about their courting.

The only vacant spot he could find turned out to be in the last pew on the left. Chantilly should be in the next one up like before, but he spotted her in the second pew from the front.

Hushed whispers abounded as people turned

around and stared at him. Folks that had known him for most of his life appeared to pity him. He didn't need anyone's pity. Couldn't they see that Daniel was wrong for Chantilly much less see him as an arrogant bastard?

Chantilly brushed a wayward strand of hair behind her ear. That's when he saw the diamond sparkling on her hand.

The woman he'd wanted his whole life had become betrothed to someone else. His chest tightened making it hard to breathe.

The choir sang. The sermon was given. But all he could focus on was the fact Daniel set his arm on the back of the bench around her when that should be him.

Well, she wasn't married yet.

The service ended. Being in the last pew, he ended up one of the first to greet the pastor. "Good to see you back again."

"Thanks."

He hustled down the steps and waited at the hitching post. Chuck, one of his friends from grade school, stopped next to him. "Sorry about Chantilly."

Blaze shrugged pretending that the whole thing didn't stink. "It's okay. With Daniel, she won't long for a thing." Except for love. He seriously doubted Daniel could love anyone but himself.

"The wife's calling me." Chuck ran toward one of

the buggies lined up on the street where a woman holding a baby waved.

He tried not to feel envious, but heck if he didn't long for a family with one beautiful gal—specifically Chantilly.

More people passed. People who looked his way either shook their heads or gave him sorrowful looks. Matt ran toward a group of teens.

Then he spotted Chantilly on Daniel's arm. He expected to see a smile gracing her mouth, not solemn indifference. She glanced at him and quickly looked away.

"Wait here. I'll get the buggy," Daniel said and strode off.

Blaze walked up behind her. "I hear congratulations are in order."

"Thank you." She wouldn't meet his eyes.

A buggy pulled up. "Excuse me, Blaze. I need to leave." She stepped away.

Daniel got out and helped her up on the seat. He eyed Blaze.

And then the buggy drove off.

"Didn't go so well, huh." Jed stood next to him.

"Nope."

"I figure any man who's more temperamental than his horses ain't worth much.'

"I totally agree. He's a bit too uppity for me." Something didn't seem right about this betrothal, and Blaze aimed to fix it before Chantilly got hurt.

CHAPTER 23

Blaze worked and didn't get to spend the next weekend in Carson City which agitated him to no end. He'd picked up the slack for a driver who took ill and ended up traveling to Lake Biggler and all the way to Sugar Loaf in California before heading back to Carson. The extra money would be great, but the timing was piss poor.

He stopped in Carson to drop off mail and exchange his horse.

Jed focused on the horse's reins. "Sorry to bear bad news but our little lassie is getting hitched on Valentine's Day."

This couldn't be true. Maybe he'd heard wrong. "Are you sure?"

"Yep. Next Friday. Two p.m."

No. No. No. He doubted he'd make it back until Friday night.

"Most of the shops will shut down for the big event."

The whole town would watch the ceremony. That's plain wrong. He should be the groom. Not that jerk. "Why the rush?"

"Don't know. Daniel's handsome and rich. He somehow charmed our lassie."

That man's as charming as a viper. She wouldn't choose Daniel if she really knew him. Numbness fogged his brain as he mounted his horse and waved goodbye.

This whole situation had become quite the mess. His horse snorted and Blaze realized he was clutching the reins far too tightly and eased up his hold.

The miles blurred as Blaze spotted the distant township of Bugsby. It looked more like a trading post and a makeshift hotel. The stables acted as a stagecoach stop and drop-off point. He wondered why the company even stopped here but supposedly there were quite a few ranches in the surrounding hills.

He kept on going until he set the mochila with mail on the hook, met up with the livery owner and changed to a new mount. This time an appaloosa.

Riding away, his mind wandered. Seeing Daniel's ring on Chantilly's finger had been plain awful.

Why would Chantilly rush into marriage? There must be an important reason.

Hell's-fire, if he hadn't been in the saloon, would he still be courting her?

The fact that Daniel had swooped right in made his gut clench. Money and power could buy just about anything, and the man obviously set his sight on her. Not that Blaze could blame him. Chantilly had always been pretty.

Still, he needed to see her again. Reason with her. Smooth things over.

Snow and sleet hit his face as the miles pounded by and the stops melded together. Stillwater. Mountain View. Middle Creek. The sky grew dark with ominous clouds, and the wind caused the American flag to sway in the wind from the top of Fort Churchill. The gates were open, and he made his way to the stables, switched his mochila, and headed on to his last stop.

Snow flurried as he reached his destination.

"Any trouble out there?" the livery owner asked.

Blaze dismounted and handed him the reins. "Nothing to complain about."

"Good to hear. Enjoy your evening."

"You, too." He took the walkway that led through the center of town. The area bustled with activity. Folks gathered in front of the store. Men smoked cigars or pipes. Miners headed into saloons.

The food had been decent at Goldie's, so he headed in that direction.

"Yippee," a miner standing with three other men shouted. He wondered what the ruckus was about. Maybe the guy hit it big or got a letter from his sweetheart.

"Howdy, Blaze."

He recognized the skinny man who sat on a bench outside. "Hello." As Blaze shook his hand, he wished he could remember the man's name. "I see the sling's gone."

The man's arm hung limply along his side. "It's healed as good as it can considering the bullet the doctor removed. Can't complain though. I'm alive."

And down on his luck given he wore tattered clothing. Making a living would be difficult without the use of one arm.

"How 'bout I buy you a meal and you can tell me your story?" He'd been in his shoes before and figured the guy might be hungry. Besides, he'd rather not eat alone.

His eyes appeared hopeful. "Deal."

"Could you tell me your name again?" He had to ask otherwise it'd be bugging him all night.

"Zeke Jones."

"All right Zeke, let's get some grub."

The two of them entered the bar and headed into a

large dining hall. The aroma of baked bread and spicy meat filled the air. Stairs led to a second story where he'd be renting a room for the night.

They were seated at a table in the middle of the room, and the server approached them. "What can I get you fellows?"

"Are you serving stew tonight?" Last week's sure had been tasty.

"Yes, we are."

"How's that sound to you?" he asked Zeke.

"Great."

"Then we'll take two bowls and coffee."

"You've got it." The young woman scurried off.

"Do you like riding for the Pony Express?" Zeke asked.

"Except for the weather, it's not bad. The days go quickly by, plus the job pays well."

"Oh, to be young again." Zeke sighed. "What do you think of Nevada?"

"Actually, I grew up in Carson City and left when my pa up and moved to Sacramento."

Zeke seemed to flinch for a second at the mention of Carson. "Gold fever, huh?

Blaze nodded.

"Thought about going myself but at the time I had a wife and child to support. Lost them both to scarlet fever. Things ain't been the same since."

"I'm sorry for your loss."

Zeke lifted a shoulder

"Have you ever been to Carson?"

Zeke's eyes widened which seemed a bit odd. "Well... about three months ago I worked for the Carson Mine... until I saw something I shouldn't have seen and got shot for it."

"What happened?"

"It's a long story."

"I've got time."

The server brought out their stew and biscuits cutting the conversation short.

Blaze buttered a bread slice and dipped it in his stew. Hmm. Zeke left town several months ago. He counted backward. That would have been the end of December or the beginning of January. "My friend, Jamey, got murdered about the same time."

Zeke's face turned ashen as he rubbed his arm. "Did you say Jamey?"

'Yeah. He owned the blacksmith shop. Did you know him?"

"Not really. He shod my horse when I first came to town. Other than that, I saw him hang out in the saloons."

"Were you in town when he was murdered?"

Zeke's posture stiffened. "You could say that."

By the way he was acting, this man knew more.

"And?" Blaze lifted a brow. "Did you see Jamey in that fateful saloon?"

"I did."

The waitress filled their coffee cups.

"Do you have any idea who might have killed him?"

Zeke gave a slight nod, then looked down at his plate.

"Is the murderer after you?"

"No, he thinks I'm dead," Zeke said in such a quiet tone it was hard to hear. He slunk down in his chair. "I haven't told a soul what occurred but it's eating me up inside. I supposed this is as good a time as any to talk."

His eyes darted around the room, as if he thought the killer might be around. "You ever witness a murder, get shot, and end up running for your life?"

"Can't say I have."

Zeke took in several deep breaths. "After a few hands of poker, I went to get some air outside and leaned against a wall under the eaves. Mind you I was hidden away just how I liked it. That's when I heard a gunshot." He let out a long sigh.

"Could you tell who was there?"

"Not at first. It looked like one man was going through the other man's pockets. I heard him shout, 'Dammit, Jamey. You said you'd bring the deed.'"

"So, Jamey was still alive?"

"Don't think so. The man pulled what looked like a

dead weight toward the wall. That's when I recognized the shooter."

"Who was it?"

Zeke shook his head.

"Please tell me. I'm friends with Jamey's sister. Her life could be in danger."

He blew out a long breath, eyed the room, and whispered, "Braddock."

Blaze sucked in a deep breath. Daniel might be arrogant, but he never thought he'd resort to murder. "Are you sure?"

"Yep. I couldn't miss the white Stetson Braddock wore when he and Jamey were gambling earlier," Zeke said.

"Never did care for the rancher. Even as a kid, he had a mean side." But Blaze hoped he'd changed. "Anyway, what occurred next? You said before you were hidden."

"I would have gone unnoticed if I hadn't sneezed. By that time, Daniel had propped Jamey on a bench. Lickety split Daniel aimed at my heart, but I saw it coming and dove away. Still, he ended up hitting me in the shoulder. It hurt like a son of a gun."

"Daniel shot you?" Blaze couldn't believe the man could be that devious.

"Sure did. The impact knocked me to the ground, but I knew I'd better get out of there or I'd be a dead man. I heard people come out of the saloon and start yelling, but I didn't pay them any mind. Luck was on my side when I spotted a wagon and climbed inside to hide."

This sounded like a dime novel. That's when an idea hit him. "Think you can make it back to Carson City this Friday?"

"The notion scares me something fierce."

"I get it. I'd be leery too. But if you don't help me, Chantilly Walsh will marry Braddock." He told Zeke about the wedding.

"I can't stand the idea of Braddock getting his hands on that sweet lady. I'm in."

The two of them came up with a plan.

The server cleared their bowls. "Are either of you interested in cinnamon strudel?"

"I'll take one." Blaze's mouth watered. He motioned to Zeke who nodded.

"Much obliged for the meal," Zeke said.

"It's my pleasure."

CHAPTER 24

"May I see the ring," the general store owner's wife asked when Chantilly visited the establishment to get some staples.

Her hand floated up as she plastered on her best smile. Daniel had been rather slick slipping the band on her finger. Since she couldn't get it off, try as she might with grease and even lard, she accepted her fate. The marriage would benefit her brother and herself, even though she wished all this hadn't occurred so fast.

"It's exquisite."

"Thank you." The enormous diamond felt ostentatious, but she did like how the stone sparkled in the sunlight. Plus, how could she fault him for being generous?

The fact that Daniel asked for Matt's approval said

he understood how much she valued family. He seemed to love her. She would grow to have the same feelings.

"Heard you two are getting hitched on Valentine's Day."

"We are."

"You're lucky to have such a thoughtful fellow. He came in earlier and had me order you a wedding gown asking for something with ivory organdy and fancy stitchery.

"Could you make it lacy?"

"Sorry, Chantilly. I already sent the requisition off to California by Pony Express."

Meaning Blaze picked up the missive. Her stomach tightened. Blaze unintentionally got involved with her wedding which seemed wrong. She strolled over to the table and fingered a floral fabric and tried to get her mind off her childhood crush. She pulled out a list from her pocket. "Think you could fill this?"

"You bet." The woman got busy pulling cans from the shelves.

"I'll send Matt or Sparky to pick this up later." On her way out the door, she ran right into those mean girls from her elementary school. "Afternoon, ladies."

"Afternoon," the ladies said together.

As she walked away, she heard one of them say, "Daniel will come to his senses."

Chantilly shook her head.

"Something troubling you?" Sparky asked as she walked into the shop and secured her apron in place.

"No."

He squinted at her. "Then why aren't you smiling? I would think you'd be excited about the upcoming nuptials."

"I am. It's just that things are happening far too quickly."

"Then slow it down. I'm sure Daniel won't mind waiting a few more months."

The problem was that Daniel would mind. After all, he mentioned how short life could be. She really should be happy. Other women would love to be engaged to such a handsome man and become the lady of his house.

"You have anything for me to do this afternoon?"

Sparky repaired an axel for a wagon. "Today's kinda quiet. Go on home and put your feet up. I'll make sure everything's locked up when I'm done."

"You're a saint." Sparky not only knew blacksmithing as well as her pa had, but he'd also become a trusted friend.

"Just so you know, Daniel stopped by and offered me a nice salary to run your shop once you're wed."

"Good to hear." Knowing Sparky would continue her family's legacy warmed her heart.

She let on a long sigh. In four days, her life would change drastically.

CHAPTER 25

Valentine's Day

An hour past dawn a courier knocked. "Package for Miss Walsh."

Matt charged to the door. "I'll get it." Her brother had been ecstatic about the wedding. In his mind, Daniel walked on water. He couldn't wait to move and live at the ranch.

Pleased for him, a part of her felt like she'd been bamboozled by both Daniel and Matt to agree to such a decision. Soon he'd be attending a university on the East Coast and studying what he loved. Once her brother left, she'd be alone on a ranch far from town with only Daniel, and unless a friend from town stopped by, her only female company would be the housekeeper.

She shook off her wayward thoughts. In a few hours, she'd be married. All financial troubles would be washed away. In theory, Daniel was the ideal husband, but in reality, her heart belonged to Blaze.

An image of Blaze came to mind. His smile made her tingle from the inside out, and when he kissed her, she'd swear she swooned.

"Here you go." Matt pressed a paper-wrapped package in her hand. "Wonder what Daniel sent this time?"

For the last week, he'd adorned her with special presents. An ivory carved hair clip. An emerald broach. Diamond teardrop earrings. Everything had been lovely, but none of the jewelry brought her joy. Unfortunately, deep inside, she just didn't love Daniel.

Her hands trembled as she opened the package. A delicate heart-shaped necklace fell into her hand.

"Don't that take the egg. Daniel sure does treat you right."

"He's a good man." Who would be her husband soon. If only her heart would start pitter-pattering at the notion.

"Let me help you with that." Matt secured the clasp around her neck.

The cold chain made her shiver. She went into her room. An ivory-colored organdy gown, embellished with tulle-embroidered flowers that Daniel had chosen, hung on a hook. A sense of sadness clenched at her heart. She'd dreamed of a gown like her mother had worn, one adorned with Chantilly lace on the collar and along the hem. This elegant gown did not have a stitch of lace.

Her hands quivered as she undid buttons on the front, slipped the garment over her head, eased her arms into the puffy sleeves, and smoothed the fitted bodice and flowing skirt in place.

She glanced in the beveled mirror above her vanity. Her skin appeared paler than usual, so she pinched her cheeks.

What else did she need for today? Gloves. She pulled the knob on the top drawer and grabbed her mother's linen gloves. An envelope fluttered to the floor.

What was this?

She read her name written in Blaze's handwriting.

Jed delivered her the note weeks ago. She'd stashed the paper in this drawer after reading it and simply forgot about it. A lacy, off-white ribbon dropped into her lap. She fingered the delicate rose pattern. Blaze's gifts might not be flashy like Daniel's, but they were thoughtful.

Quit comparing, she chastised herself. The fact she'd be marrying Daniel in less than an hour didn't stop her from opening the envelope once again.

. . .

Dear Tilly,

The lacy ribbon makes me think of you. Beautiful. Intriguing. Full of life.

I love how your eyes light up when you are enthralled. I love your stubbornness and tenacious strength. I love you.

Please give me another chance.

Loving regards,

Blaze

He really loves me. Her pulse sped fast, recalling how his touch made her insides turned to mush. Still, she couldn't take a chance with him. Daniel was the right choice.

She brushed her long locks, twisted her hair up into a chignon, and stared at her reflection in the mirror. Picking up the ribbon, she toyed with the silky length wishing things could be different and she'd married Blaze instead of Daniel.

It seemed wrong to wear a gift from another man, so she dropped the ribbon on top of the vanity.

She stared in the mirror. Longing for what might have been. Her eyes misted with tears. Tears she hadn't shed since her brother died. She picked up a handkerchief from the vanity's top and dabbed the drip with the lacy square. The one Blaze had given her on their first date.

Blaze loves me.

Push away the thought. I've chosen Daniel.

A bushel of doubt dropped into her middle. This marriage would be for the rest of her life. Angst twisted in her stomach.

Daniel loves me, too. He owns his own ranch. She wouldn't have to worry about him getting killed delivering mail and abandoning her like the others. She straightened her shoulders. Today, she would become Daniel's wife.

"May I come in?" Matt asked from the other side of the door.

"Please." After today, this room would no longer be hers.

Her brother looked ever so handsome in the tailored suit Daniel provided. "Golly, sis. You sure are pretty." Her brother's colossal grin gave her enough proof she'd made the right choice. In a few months, he'd be living his dream, and all because she'd be marrying Daniel.

She stood and smoothed out her dress. Her eyes got misty. The heck with propriety. She tied the handkerchief around her wrist with the ribbon.

"You ready?" He hugged her tight.

"I am." They walked out into the living room.

Her brother helped her with her new hooded sheepskin jacket lined with rabbit fur.

She glanced around the living room where she'd lived for so many years. This cabin had been filled with love and laughter. The ghosts of her past came to her. Pa smoking his pipe, Ma rocking little Matt, while she and Jamey argued over whose turn it was to spin the top. Home sweet home, Ma had called it.

As she closed the door and locked it, she fought off a twist of wistfulness. Standing tall and determined to let go of any melancholy, she told herself she would always have her memories.

She stared at the boxy storefront and remembered how Pa beamed when he hung the Walsh's Blacksmith Shop sign. "This is our legacy. One that will live on for generations," he'd said with such high hopes.

At the livery, Jed had a coach ready. He helped her into the back seat."

Her old friend would escort her down the aisle. She refused to look him in the eye. "I'm marrying Daniel."

"Why aren't you smiling?" Matt eased into the driver's spot on her left as Jed moved to her right.

"Wedding jitters." The words came out with confidence as worry nagged the back of her mind. She shivered but not from the cold air.

CHANTILLY CLUTCHED Matt's arm as she walked toward the whitewashed chapel and stared up at the cross on top of the steeple. The idea of God watching her almost made her chuckle. He'd forsaken her long ago.

Her shoes clicked up the steps.

"I couldn't ask for a better sister." Matt kissed her cheek. "You deserve to be happy."

"I am."

She peered inside the open door. Folks from clear across the territory jammed into sixteen pews on both sides of the church. She knew there were sixteen because she'd counted them plenty of times over the years when she got bored during a sermon.

Matt waved to the organist at the side of the altar.

The first notes of the "Wedding March" played and everyone stood. Some appeared jubilant. Others gawked. A few of the women her age seemed to sneer. Clutching Matt's arm tightly, she fidgeted with the lace handkerchief tied with the ribbon on the end of her wrist. Another reminder of Blaze she couldn't quite let go. The item somehow gave her comfort.

Matt raised a concerned eyebrow. "You sure you want to do this?"

"Of course." She corralled any protest with a brilliant smile.

Daniel waited up front with the preacher. His chin

held high and standing tall. Confident in his dark pin-striped suit and white Stetson.

One step. Two steps. Three, four, five, six, seven steps. She couldn't help counting each one until she reached the front and stood facing Daniel.

His gloved hands took both of hers. "You look stunning, Chant."

Chant made her think of chanting a line or limerick. This isn't the time to let him know the nickname bothered her. She'd tell him after they married.

Her eyes drifted to the right side of his pants. An ivory-edged pistol peeked above one of the black leather double-holsters.

"Dearly Beloved," the pastor repeated the same line he'd said at Jamey's funeral, except this time with a bit more jubilance. "We are gathered here in the presence of these witnesses to join Daniel Braddock and Chantilly Walsh in holy matrimony. I'm sure you all agree Valentine's Day is a fitting time to commit their love to the Almighty."

Murmurs of agreement sounded. The preacher continued on. She caught words and phrases like, sanctity of vows, for richer, for poorer, to love and cherish and obey, and until death do us part.

Could she really learn to love him? Everyone grew quiet.

Daniel squeezed her hand and mouthed for her to speak.

"I do."

Daniel slid a gold band on her right ring finger as a symbol of their bond.

"I now pronounce you man and wife," the preacher called. "You may kiss the bride."

Daniel wrapped his arms around her waist and brought his mouth down to hers with a soft kiss. It suddenly hit her that from now on she'd be sleeping in Daniel's bed. Forever she'd be Daniel's wife. A cold chill shivered through her body.

"Mrs. Braddock, you've made me one happy man." Daniel let go of her waist.

She just forced a smile. What else could she do?

Boot steps clicked at the back.

She swiveled.

Blaze?

"Stop the wedding," he strutted to the middle of the aisle and shouted.

Her pulse rushed through her veins at the sight of him. She'd already married another man. It didn't matter that she loved Blaze, she'd promised to be a good wife to Daniel.

CHAPTER 26

Blaze huffed as he ran up the stairs to the chapel hoping he wasn't too late. Nothing had gone as planned. He'd had a long day yesterday adding in two extra stops and shortening his stops for today to three. This action should have allowed him enough time to get to Carson City well before the wedding. Unfortunately, he could hear the church bell ring as he got to the outskirts of town.

Galloping down Main Street, he had to slow and then finally stop when he saw people crossing the street. All the while tapping his hand against his leg.

Finally, he made it. Dismounting at the entrance, he nodded at Zeke who stood at the bottom. He'd agreed to wait outside until Blaze called for him.

Rushing up the steps, Blaze pushed the door open.

The sound of wood thudded against the wall. Faces turned and gawked at him, but he put his focus on the front of the church where Chantilly faced Daniel.

"Stop the wedding," his baritone voice boomed across the room.

"Mail boy, I am Chantilly's choice. Not you." Daniel pointed to the sheriff near the back. "Kindly remove this man."

The sheriff stood and took Blaze's arm. "Come along, Blaze."

"I can't go until Chantilly learns Daniel murdered her brother." Blaze clenched his fists and dug his heels into the ground.

"You killed Jamey?" She yanked her right hand away, but not her left.

"How could you question me, Chant? Jamey was my best friend. I miss him every day."

Chantilly's wide eyes begged Blaze to give her a reason.

"I have proof," Blaze's words echoed inside the quiet room.

"What evidence? You have nothing against me."

"Zeke Thomas says differently."

"Zeke who works in the mines?" someone shouted.

"He's the man. Daniel aimed to kill him but missed and hit his shoulder."

Several people in the crowd gasped. Others murmured to their neighbor.

"That's blasphemy, Sheriff. Everyone knows I'm an upstanding citizen." Daniel rocked on his heels as his upper lip curled up with a mock smile.

"What I say is true." Blaze motioned for a gray-haired man at the door to step forward. "Sheriff, I think you're gonna want to hear what Zeke has to say."

"I'll have no part of this. Come on, Chant." Daniel tugged on her hand. "Let's get out of here. We have a celebration to attend with our guests." Deep red colored his face.

"Stay right where you are, Braddock." The sheriff held up his hand. "Mr. Thomas, what do you have to say?"

Blaze didn't trust the rancher, so he kept his eyes fixed on him. That's when he spotted the double holster. Daniel's free hand twitched on the handle of a gun.

"It all started in the wee hours after Christmas. I came out of the Silver Dollar Saloon to get some air and leaned against a wall under the eaves back corner of the building when I heard a gunshot."

"Meaning he was drunk. His account is nothing but a bunch of nonsense." Daniel tugged Chantilly even tighter against his side.

"I only had two shots of rotgut the whole night. Anyway, there was enough moonlight to see that guy going through the fellow's pockets." He pointed to Daniel.

"This is balderdash," Daniel huffed.

"Braddock, let the man tell his story," the sheriff hollered.

"It's true. Braddock always wears a white Stetson. As he got closer, I could tell he was dragging his gambling buddy. Jamey wasn't moving."

"Quite the storyteller. You're nothing but an old drunk." Daniel gave a dismissive chortle.

"And you're a killer. When I sneezed, you spotted me, turned your gun, and hit me with a bullet in the shoulder. Hurt like the dickens but I was not about to stick around and let you kill me too."

"How much did Blaze pay you to tell such lies?" Daniel chuffed.

"It's the God's honest truth," Zeke called out.

CHAPTER 27

"You killed my brother? Why?" The man Chantilly just married murdered her brother in cold blood. This whole ordeal seemed unreal.

"I'd like to know the same thing," her brother shouted.

"So would I," she heard other people murmur.

"It's a bunch of lies. You know that me and Jamey were friends. I miss him just as much as you." Still facing her, his voice got low and filled with a warning to not challenge him.

"I don't believe you."

"How can you say that? I've always been good to you and your family."

She noticed the pistol in his free hand and held back a scream while her legs trembled in trepidation.

"Come on, Chant. It's time for our wedding celebration." He snagged her around the waist. She tried to move away but he held firm.

"You're hurting me, Daniel. Let me go."

He gripped her even tighter. "You're mine."

Matt rushed up the aisle toward her. "Let my sister go."

"Never."

"Back away, Matt." Fear shot through her veins like a slingshot. Her stomach churned making her want to retch. But she had to keep her wits and figure a way out of this mess. At this moment she couldn't chance that Daniel might shoot her brother.

"I don't like it," Matt grumbled.

"Please," she caught eyes with her brother. "Do this for me."

Matt's eyes widened with concern as he edged back a few steps.

Thank God he listened.

"Now if you'll excuse us, me and the missus will be on our way," Daniel spoke quickly.

"You're not going anywhere," the sheriff said in a no-nonsense tone.

"I'm the one who makes the calls, sheriff." Daniel waved his pistol in the air, pulled the trigger, and fired.

She glanced at the crowd. Folks crouched behind pews. A couple in the back row snuck out the door.

The sheriff picked up his rifle, but Daniel turned his gun on him.

"Drop the gun, sheriff or I'll shoot." He pointed the barrel at Matt.

The sheriff set his rifle on the floor and held his hands up. "Come on, Daniel. We need to talk this out reasonably."

"No, we don't. You're well aware that I make the rules around here." Daniel pushed her forward.

"I'm not going," she hissed.

The gun's trigger clicked in place. "I'd think twice about that," he whispered in her ear and aimed the pistol toward Matt.

How had she not realized what a monster he was before this? Taking a steadying breath, she whispered, "Fine."

"Good girl." He tightened his grip on her. "Nobody follows us or she's dead." He tapped her temple with the barrel of the gun for emphasis. "Me n' the missus are going to start our honeymoon early. Wife, my buggy's out front." Daniel's menacing tone could freeze hell. "No funny moves."

They made it down the steps. Still gripping her waist tightly, he took his gun away from her head and held it at his side as he kept eyeing the area.

"Why'd you kill Jamey?" The thought that this man

now held control of her made her livid. She deserved answers.

He snarled, "Learned there's a mighty rich silver vein in the hills behind your cabin, and I had to get my hands on it."

"You did this for silver?"

"Sure did," he growled.

"So, you killed my brother to get him out of the way?"

"Yep." He gave her a maniacal laugh.

This man was unhinged.

"Jamey owed me the deed." He pushed her forward.

"Why did you need it? You don't need money."

"Never said I did. But I want it. Like I want *you*. When I saw you at the funeral, I came up with another plan. You know I'd always hankered to have you. Jamey told me to stay away, acting like you were too good for the likes of me."

She couldn't stop the shiver climbing up her spine. In his own sick way, he really liked her.

Matt's words, *He's sweet on you,* took on a new meaning.

"I figured I could lure you to marry me by offering to help Matt."

She tried to sink in her heels as they moved toward his brand-new two-seater buggy, but he dragged her forward. One of the two black stallions snorted reminding her that the combined strength of both horses would be hard to catch. She had to get away from Daniel before it was too late. But how? Her mind whirled but not with ideas, it whirled with thoughts of what he'd do when he got her alone.

"You won't get away with this. Everyone knows what you did."

"Shut up, wife. You're my property now." His grip remained on her waist while his gun aimed for the door of the church and anyone who might exit. Panic threatened to overwhelm her, and her legs trembled. She had to save herself.

"Get up there." He motioned with his head.

Eyeing the buggy as he let go of her, she came up with a plan. She scooted all the way to the side and jumped off, only to have her wrist ensnared by him. She bit his hand so hard she could taste his blood in her mouth.

"You bitch." He dropped his hold and shouted, "I'm gonna kill you!"

Scared out of her wits, she sprinted as fast as she could toward the church when a gunshot sounded. She expected to feel pain as a bullet embedded into her back, but she felt nothing. Not about to slow her pace as she reached the church steps, she raced up keeping her eyes on her destination so as not to trip, opened the door, and found herself barreling into a solid wall of a man.

"Thank God you're all right," Blaze said as he wrapped her in a warm embrace. "Did Daniel harm you in any way?"

"I think he might have shot me although I don't feel anything?" Spots formed in her eyes but she forced herself to stay lucid. Now was not the time to pass out. "Maybe he missed."

Blaze picked her up in his arms, setting her on a front pew and examining her for wounds. "I don't see any blood," he said.

Her head got woozy, and her body started trembling. She could have died.

"I'll guard the door in case Braddock tries to get inside," Zeke rushed off with a rifle in hand.

"Are you okay?" Matt plopped onto the bench on the other side of her and took her hand in his.

"I'm fine."

"Thank God." He closed his eyes and let out a long sigh. "I was so worried."

"So was I," she laughed, not about to shed any tears in front of him.

"I know I can be a bit ungrateful, Chantilly, but I love you. I couldn't live without you."

"I love you, too, Matty." She decided to use the nickname she called him when he was little.

That's when she noticed people milling around inside.

A loud banging sounded on the door. "It's safe out here. Everyone is free to leave." The sheriff marched inside.

"Did Daniel get away?" somebody asked.

"Nope."

"Did you arrest him?" another person else shouted

"Not exactly. I snuck out the back door and saw Daniel about to shoot Miss Walsh. I couldn't let that ensue, so I fired."

So that was the blast she heard.

"Is he dead?" Matt asked.

"Sure is."

"I want to see for myself." Chantilly stood.

"I don't think it's a good idea," Blaze said, but she didn't care and started walking. He placed his arm around her shoulders. "You're not going anywhere without me."

"Me either." Matt strode beside her, and they made their way outside.

She noticed a body on the ground near the buggies and horses. He lay still. His blue eyes lifeless. This was surreal. She'd just said her vows to Daniel. She'd thought him a good man. Not a murderer.

He killed Jamey for supposed silver in the hills. Her mouth went dry.

How could he do such a thing?

Well, he got his comeuppance.

She should feel relief. Not utter sadness for this man. "I don't get it. He had everything, and it wasn't enough.

"Some people choose the wrong path." Blaze pulled her closer.

"I'm sorry, sis," Matt said, and she noticed how his chin wobbled. "I wanted to go to a university and pushed you to be with Daniel. I was wrong."

"It's not your fault. He fooled us all," she added and moved toward her brother to grasp his hands as she faced him. "You did what you thought was right at the time. We have each other. That won't change."

"I love you, sis." Matt's eyes shone with tenderness.

"I love you, too."

The preacher walked out and covered Daniel's body with a quilt. "May he rest in peace."

"Amen," she said as did others. As fearful as she had been a part of her hoped he'd find salvation.

"Oh dear, God, Daniel's dead," a woman said. "It's so sad."

"Looks like he'll be joining the rest of his family," someone else replied.

"Not if he murdered Jamey. I wonder if he murdered others. Maybe even his parents."

"That's blasphemy. Daniel was a generous boss."

"Quit talking ill of the dead. Daniel did a great deal for our community."

The conversations were getting to her along with the craziness she'd just experienced. "I'd like to sit if it's okay."

"Of course." Blaze said, his eyes wide with concern.

"I'm fine. Really. "As fine as anyone could be who got married and almost kidnapped all in the same hour. She could have died or—a shudder shimmied through her whole body thinking about what Daniel would have done to her once he got her alone. She held Blaze's arm in her right Matt's in her left as they led her to a quiet spot towards the back of the chapel.

Flynn walked over to them. "Let me know if you need anything."

"Thanks," Chantilly smiled at the older man.

"I could use a distraction. You have any animals that need caring?" Matt asked.

"As a matter of fact, I do. Farmer Jones has a mare that's about to foal. Do you want to join me?"

And just like that Matt was trailing after Flynn.

She turned to Blaze. "Let's go home."

"You've got it."

They held hands as they made their way to the blacksmith's shop.

Her voice caught as hot tears flowed down her cheeks. "I made a colossal mistake pushing you away. I was so afraid you'd end up like Jamey and abandon me."

"Never, my sweet Tilly."

"And to be honest, I was afraid I'd lose Matt, too. He was following in Jamey's footsteps. Daniel promised a better future for him."

"I understand."

They reached her home. "Would you mind if we sit over their under that tree?"

"Not at all."

Blaze sat next to her, placing his arm around her shoulders. "We're lucky. It's over now. Daniel's gone for good."

"Thank the Lord." They sat there for several minutes listening to the birds chirp as she relaxed in his arms. "This morning, I found your letter again. It said you love me."

"That will never change."

A flutter of white tumbled to the ground. Blaze picked it up and chuckled. "I can't believe you went to the altar with my handkerchief."

CHAPTER 28

It took plenty of persuasion to get Blaze to do his route on Monday. After all that Chantilly had been through, he hadn't wanted to leave her. But she insisted he go and he reluctantly agreed to take the next route.

Thus, on her first day home, Chantilly cocooned herself from the outside world in her cabin all day, avoiding comments and the aftermath of the wedding. She tried to convince Matt to do the same, but he said he would be just fine. The idea that there was a second part of the deed drove her crazy. Maybe Jamey or her father hid it somewhere in the house, so she spent Monday searching. She did the same thing on Tuesday morning until it was time to work in the shop. By that evening, she went through every nook and cranny with no luck.

Wednesday after work she explored the hills, but with so much land and no hint of where silver might be found, she gave up.

Thursday, she attended the funeral wearing all black. Most of the town came and she could tell several of the women were gossiping about her and Matt, but she held her head high.

Friday morning the ordeal was finally over. Now that she'd finished with breakfast and sent Matt off to school, she searched the house, going through books and wardrobes, before sitting at the desk in the living room and sifting through the drawers one more time. Taking everything out of the top one, she noticed a small panel covering the center. She used a letter opener to nudge it off. Inside she found two folded papers.

Excitement thrummed through her veins.

The first document turned out to be page two of the deed which listed the property details including a drawing of the parcel. The second paper had the words *Silver Map* written on top. Her fingers trembled as she opened a hand-drawn map of her property with an X next to a cave in the foothills where she and Jamey used to play chase.

Did this come from Pa or Jamey, and why didn't either of them tell her about this?

A soft tap rapped on the front door.

"Who is it?" she called.

"William from Clark's Law. I have a letter for you."

She undid the lock.

What if it was bad news? Curiosity had her biting her bottom lip. *You won't know till you open it.*

She pulled open the wax seal.

Chantilly Braddock,

Your presence is required at Clark's Law Office on Friday, February 19, 1861, on the hour, 10 o'clock.

Sincerely,

Samuel Clark

Attorney at Law

What the heck could Mr. Clark want with her? The formality of this missive caused a prickling on the back of her head.

Instinct had her walking over to the livery to show this to Jeb.

"I'm expected at Samuel Clark's Law Office." She handed the note to the older gentleman. "I don't understand why it lists my surname as Braddock. What do you think this is about?"

"You married Daniel in front of God and plenty of witnesses. You're his widow," Jed said firmly.

His widow. She considered the marriage over when Daniel died.

Not wanting to go alone, she asked Jed, "Would you mind escorting me?"

"I'd be more than happy to join you." He gave her a broad smile.

THE CLOCK TOWER chimed ten times as Chantilly was led into the lawyer's office with Jed at her side. Sitting in a hard wooden chair, her muscles twitched.

A tall, thin man with dark hair stood. "Mrs. Braddock, I'm sorry for your loss."

"Thank you," her voice squeaked. Samuel Clark had been at her wedding along with most of the town and witnessed what happened.

"Please be seated," he motioned to her and Jed.

"What is going on Mr. Clark?"

"It is my duty to discuss the Braddock estate and inform you of your legal obligations."

She nodded unsure exactly what this meant.

"The case is rather unique. You see, I asked Daniel to draw up a will upon his engagement to you." He paused and looked at her. "The estate leaves everything to his next of kin."

"And who might that be?"

"Given that you are legally married, you inherit everything."

"Everything?" She must have heard wrong.

"Yes, ma'am."

Did he just say she inherited all of Daniel's property? She settled back in her chair, threaded her fingers together, and stared at her hands.

"Exactly what is included in the estate?" Jed asked.

Samuel shuffled through some papers. "Here it is. According to the latest document, the property includes the estate, a thousand acres, cattle, horses, water, and mineral rights."

"My goodness. All of that is mine?" It just didn't seem possible.

"You have some decisions to make as to which staff you plan to employ. Daniel's foreman can fill you in."

"I've known the foreman, Christopher for years. He's a hard worker and straightforward." Jed squeezed her hand.

Just like that, Chantilly went from a blacksmith's daughter to a wealthy rancher.

She looked upward and figured Jamey was smiling down on her.

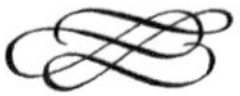

CHAPTER 29

Blaze knocked on Chantilly's door, ready to have a serious talk about their future.

Matt opened it. "Boy, do we have some things to tell you."

"All good I hope." After last week, Blaze didn't need more adversity.

"Sure is. Come on in." Chantilly motioned him over to the kitchen table.

"And I've got news for you."

"Have a seat.

"All right." He kissed her cheek. "Did you find that silver vein on your property?"

"No. Although I did go exploring."

He had to say his piece. "Mind if I go first?" His

throat went dry with nerves. "I've been waiting all week to talk with you."

"But what I've got to say is quite amazing."

"Please, Tilly." He toyed with a lock of her hair.

"Fine," she sighed.

"On the road all I could think about was you." A surge of adrenaline thrummed through his veins. Might as well get this over with. "This might be sudden, but one thing I've learned, life can be unpredictable. I don't want to waste another minute without letting you know how much you mean to me. I love you, Chantilly. Always have."

"I love you, too."

He dropped to one knee and took the ring out of his pocket. The fact he didn't fumble with the band was a miracle because of how much his hands were shaking. "Life means nothing without you at my side. I don't want to wait another moment without you knowing what's in my heart."

She tilted her head to the side as her eyes brimmed with tears.

He couldn't stop now. "Make me the happiest man on Earth, Tilly, and marry me."

A huge grin graced her face.

"Wait a minute." Her brow crinkled as her mouth dropped. "What I have to say might change our future."

"If you're worried about where we'll live, I'm

thinking about putting in an offer on a ranch near Egan Canyon that's been vacant for several years."

She bit her bottom lip.

"You don't want to live on a ranch?" He hadn't really discussed her ideal location to live but assumed she'd be pleased with the notion of their place. "I mean, if you don't want to move, I could help out with the blacksmith shop. All I care about is being with you."

"My gosh, you're cute when you're nervous." She laced her fingers through his.

"Well, are you gonna put me out of my misery?" He remained on one knee. Still with no answer. The room was unbearably quiet.

"Did you forget I'm a widower?" She pressed her lips together.

Dang if his heart didn't stop right there. "You married Daniel but never well …" He stopped. "Are you saying you're in mourning?"

"Not exactly. I now own the Double-B Ranch."

"Own it?"

"Every lock, stock, and barrel of the thousand acres." She flipped her braid behind her back. "I inherited Daniel's cattle ranch. He was an only child who lost his parents several years ago. According to the lawyer, I married him, and it was legitimate before he died. I'm the heir."

"Are you joshing with me?" His throat choked up.

" I figure getting the ranch is the least Daniel could do for me after murdering Jamey." Her voice came out small and tinny. "Are you all right marrying a wealthy woman?"

He let out a long breath. She still wanted him. "As long as it's you."

"Then I say yes, yes, a thousand times yes."

He pulled her into his arms for a kiss. One that showed just how happy she made him.

Matt clapped. "Congratulations, sis."

Blazed glanced at her brother. "I should have asked for your permission."

"The smile on her face says you'll be good for her." He puffed up a little taller. "But you'd better treat her right."

"I promise."

"I thought I had everything figured out for our future. And you, my dear, just upped the ante." He brushed his lips against hers. "You're full of surprises.

"I'm still numb, and I've known about this for two days."

"What are you going to do with the ranch?"

"I'm not certain. After the horrible things Daniel put us through, my first thought had been to sell the place."

"But?" Blaze asked.

"I believe with the ranch we can make a different for our town and the surrounding areas. Plus, I'd hate to see someone buy the property and use it for mining, putting the ranch hands and others out of a job. I think Jamey would approve."

Blaze nodded. Still unsure of where he fit in this scheme.

"You wanted a ranch. This place would be perfect. That is if I have some help." Her eyes danced as she spoke.

"I'll help you during the summer," Matt chimed in. "Think I could invite some of my friends over once we get settled?"

"Absolutely." She turned to Blaze. "There's one more question I need to ask. Would you consider moving there?"

"I want to be anywhere you are." He couldn't stop grinning. A week ago, he had lost his gal. Now they were getting married.

"What are you smiling about?"

"I'm just glad to be with you."

"Talk about corny." Matt let out a sigh.

"I'm not complaining." He pulled her onto his lap, needing the closeness of her. Blaze couldn't resist giving her a long kiss that showed how much she meant to him.

"Can you two quit that mushy stuff?" Matt grimaced, turned away, and added a log into the fireplace.

"Never," Blaze continued kissing her grateful he'd arrived in time to save his childhood love.

She held her emerald up to the light to admire the sparkles. "Where'd you find the ring?"

"Saw it in a shop window at Fort Churchill. The green reminds me of your expressive eyes."

"Such a charmer." She touched a hand to her heart.

"How soon can we get hitched?"

"I'd do it tomorrow, but given all that transpired I think we should wait at least thirty days and maybe two months."

"What about June so I'll be home for the summer?" Matt asked.

"Would that be okay?" She turned to him.

"I can wait as long as we're together." His heart sang at the thought.

"When are you moving out to the ranch?"

"Tomorrow."

"That soon?" he squeezed her hand. "Do you want me to keep working for the Pony Express until we wed?"

"I'd rather have you stay with me. I love you so, Blaze." Her arms flung around his shoulders.

"I love you, too." They kissed for the longest time.

And just like that his plans had changed for the better.

CHAPTER 30

On June 4th, Chantilly and Blaze rode in the back bench of a four-seater buggy ready to enjoy a quiet wedding in the southeast town of Genoa.

In a few minutes, she'd be saying her vows once again. This time to the man she loved with her whole heart.

She fiddled with her hat, not at all nervous about tying the knot, but eager.

Blaze put his arm around her shoulder. "Soon, you'll be my bride."

She couldn't wait to say her vows. Blaze was her hero. If it hadn't been for him, she might not have ever learned the truth.

"We're here." Matt pulled the buggy past the

hitching post in front of the rocked walkway leading to the entrance.

Blaze's hand rested on hers. "I love you," he whispered.

Three little words and her heart radiated with joy.

"Are you ready?" Matt opened the door, helped her out of the buggy, and handed her a box with her dress in it from the back.

"More than anything." She had no qualms about Blaze.

"Good." Matt trotted up the steps to the entrance.

Blaze took her hand and escorted her to the foyer. She counted the pews. Old habit. Four pews on each side. Totaling eight.

Jed motioned Blaze to join him at the left side, still, she overheard their conversation. "She's like a daughter to me. Make her happy."

"I will."

Chantilly had no doubt Blaze would honor the request.

The pastor's wife came through the chapel's door. "Let's get you gussied

up."

"I really appreciate you helping me." She thought about her mother who always liked Blaze. How she wished she could be here.

"It's my pleasure."

She followed the woman into a side room and got out her dress."

The woman opened the box. "That's gotta be the purdiest gown I've ever seen."

Finding the wedding gown was as if her mother's angel led Matt to a chest in the rafters of their cabin. He got it down and brought it into her room. Underneath a worn patchwork comforter, she pulled out the dress. Moths had chewed a couple of holes in the hem, which she darned in less than an hour.

"It was my mother's." She recalled how Ma's eyes sparkled as she talked about her wedding gown and how she loved the lace that adorned the bodice and top layer of the skirt. Glancing into the long mirror, she knew her mother would approve.

"You look fetching. If your fellow isn't already smitten, this gown will do the trick."

"Thank you." With the way he gazed at her during the ride here, she hoped to dazzle him.

Several minutes later, she was led to the foyer of the chapel and took Jed's arm. "I'm happy for you," he whispered.

The pastor's wife moved to the front and played the "Wedding March" on a piano.

Matt stood tall and stoic in his Sunday best, a dress shirt and pants. As Blaze's best man, he obviously took his job seriously.

Then her eyes collided with Blaze's. His love for her shone like a beacon of hope and promise. And that grin, the one that showed the dimples in his cheeks, nearly made her swoon.

It took restraint not to run to him. When Jed passed her over to Blaze and their fingers clasped, she could swear that she heard clapping from the heavens above.

The pastor opened his bible and moved his wire-rimmed glasses up on his nose. "We are gathered here together to join Chantilly Walsh with Blaze Steele in holy matrimony."

Blaze held her hand all the while, smiling at her, and she couldn't help smiling right back.

"Do you, Chantilly Walsh, promise to love, honor, and obey, till death do you part?"

She held up one hand. As much as she wanted to be Blaze's wife, she needed clarification. "I'm fine with loving and honoring my husband. As far as I'm concerned, obeying needs to be on both sides."

Jed and Matt chuckled.

"That's my girl." Blaze let out a loud guffaw.

"Looks like your little wife's got spirit. This will make for an interesting marriage."

"I'm counting on it." He leaned over and kissed her cheek.

His simple touch had her quivering with need and more than ready for the wedding night.

AUTHOR'S NOTE

Author's Note

The Pony Express lasted from April 1860 to October 1861. The hardy men used a relay system that could carry mail from Missouri to California in just ten days. The need for fast mail service past the Rockies was a result of thousands of people migrating west along the Oregon Trail beginning in 1840, the 1847 Mormon exodus to Utah, and the California Gold Rush in 1849.

The rides could be treacherous killing seven men before the end of the service. The men had to deal with winter storms and extreme heat while riding anywhere from seventy-five to a hundred miles a day.

I chose Carson City for the story because of its rich history. The Comstock Lode started in the neighboring town of Virginia City in 1858. Carson City became the state capital in November of 1861.

Since this is fiction, I took several liberties with facts.

For more about the Pony Express, the National Pony Express Association is full of fun facts and maps.

https://nationalponyexpress.org/historic-pony-express-trail/stations/

TIME TO SAVE A COWBOY

If you enjoyed HER PONY EXPRESS HERO, you might want to read TIME TO SAVE A COWBOY from my Western Romance Time Travel Series.

Captivated by the story of a cowboy hanged as a horse thief in 1890, Mia Kellogg travels back in time with only thirty days to save an innocent man.

Dusty Mann is determined to buy his own ranch.

He doesn't need a modern, straightforward woman to barrel into his life or knock his plans off track.

But Mia steals his heart—and then says she's from the future.

Read the first chapter from TIME TO SAVE A COWBOY

TIME TO SAVE A COWBOY
CHAPTER 1

Time to Save a Cowboy

Present Day, Old Town Rialto, California

The sepia photograph of a cowboy in the antique shop's window drew Amelia Kellogg closer. For the moment, she shut out the clamor of people and the bustling noise and stared at the man in the dark Stetson. His bronze complexion. His square chin shadowed with dark stubble gave him a handsome rugged quality. His lips pinched together as if he tried to stay serious. And failed.

Her cousin's floor-length skirt swished as she stepped next to Mia. "What are you looking at?" Birdie tilted her head. The pink ostrich feather in her old-fashioned knob-shaped hat quivered.

"This guy's gorgeous." Mia did a Vanna sweep of her hands to the picture. His direct gaze mixed with playfulness and confidence "It seems like he's staring right at me."

"You do realize it's only a picture."

"Way to ruin my fantasy." Mia let out an exaggerated sigh. Underneath her long taffeta dress, her corset pinched her waist. Her cousin had cinched her strings so tightly Mia could hardly breathe, while insisting their costumes looked authentic for their trip on a turn-of-the-century steam locomotive.

"You need to get out more."

Birdie had a point. For the past few years, Mia's career came first, ruining her last few relationships. She didn't need a man to be happy, but she definitely needed this mini vacation on a nineteenth century steam locomotive.

Her focus drifted back to the photo. What kind of life had this cowboy led? She imagined a hint of longing or heartache in his expression. *Crazy. Now I'm making up a life story for this guy.*

Antique bottles and glassware were placed on shelves below the picture in the window. It made her wonder about other treasures the shop might have inside.

"Let's go in. I want to check it out." Birdie pushed open the door and bells chimed.

"We'll miss our train."

Birdie glanced at the time on her phone. "It's only quarter to one. We have forty-five minutes before the train even arrives."

"All right, ten minutes." Mia strolled inside the cluttered room, fingered a hand-blown glass vase, then picked up a porcelain cat figurine. "Too bad the paw broke off. It's cute."

"I suppose." Birdie scrunched her nose. "This room smells like dirty socks and moth balls." The scent didn't stop her cousin from wandering toward a pile of children's books, grabbing one, blowing off the dust and leafing through the pages. "Look, an original *Dick and Jane.*"

"Nice." A text-message beeped. Mia grabbed her phone.

Congrats. You're in charge of the Cashmere Kitty website.

The account came with an ultra-demanding client. She stifled a groan.

"What's the matter?"

"A work thing." Mia shook her head. "But we're in partying mode. No stress for the next forty-eight hours." She clicked off her cell.

Birdie rested her hand on Mia's shoulder. "It's about time you relax and have fun."

"Fun?" Mia's upper lip twitched.

"You know, being amused, happy, entertained."

"Sounds kinda familiar." Mia giggled. "I'm gonna see if there's any jewelry."

"Go ahead. I'll meet up with you." Birdie waved her on.

As Mia strolled into a long musty room, a current of mystery stirred the air. On the wall, a variety of coiled ropes hung on horseshoe nails. She passed a saddle on a stand and headed for a glass display case. Incandescent light gleamed off shiny trinkets. A rusted pistol, knives sheathed in leather, spurs, a silver belt buckle, gold-hooped earrings, a cracked cameo. Nothing of interest.

An older gentleman popped up from behind the counter. "May I help you?"

She jumped, and her pulse warped to fast lane speed.

"Sorry to have startled you." He twisted the silver ends of his mustache. "I was busy cleaning out a bottom drawer over there. Thought I heard footsteps."

Still a bit spooked, she fidgeted with her purse.

"May I help you find anything in particular?"

"You have something to go with my ruby earrings?"

"I may have just the thing for you. This ring came in yesterday." He reached behind on a shelf and produced a small black box with a fancy golden latch. His long fingers carefully opened the container, as he moved it over for her to see. "The previous owner said the ring has been in the family for several centuries. Supposed to fire up the heart for love," he said in a quiet voice.

"I don't believe in superstitious things." Although she liked watching paranormal movies.

"It makes a fun story. We get all kinds. A man brought in that rusted gun; said it was cursed. People say just about anything to try to get a better price."

"I can imagine." She couldn't blame the seller. When money's tight, you do what you can to survive.

"Would you like to try the ring on?"

"Yes, please." She slipped the thin gold band shimmering with inlaid rubies on her finger—it fit perfectly. Then she turned the case over and saw the price. Hmm … two-hundred dollars was a steal but only if the stones were real. "Do you have a certificate of authenticity to prove it's ruby?"

"No. I'm going by what I was told. Our appraiser won't be in 'till next week."

She held it up to the light and noted the deep red color. "It's garnet, not ruby." Taking the ring off, she placed it back in the case. She didn't need the ring, but wanted it, and asked, "Would you take a hundred?"

"One twenty-five's the lowest I can go."

She'd consider it a souvenir from this trip. "Okay, I'll take it."

"Excellent choice."

The superstition behind the ring would make a great tale to tell her friends.

The man carried the box to the front and rung up the sale. On the counter, a frayed scrapbook lay open to a newspaper clipping with an etching of a cowboy. She edged in close enough to recognize the same man from the window photo.

The clerk handed her the purchase, and she slipped her ring inside her purse.

"Interesting article. The same person with your ring brought in this scrapbook and the photo in the window."

Hesperia Weekly Press, July 6th, 1890
Local Foreman, Dusty Mann, Hanged as Horse Thief.

Her heart saddened at the caption.

Los Flores Ranch, Hesperia, California, 1890

The horse's long shadow against the flat desert landscape signaled the last speck of day. Dusty's gut gurgled, telling him to hurry back to the ranch's dining hall or there'd be nothing left.

Fifty yards away a calf struggled, his leg caught in a barbed wire fence. Dusty dismounted, untangled the wounded calf, and slipped a noose around the frightened animal's neck. It kicked, nicking Dusty's shin. "Ouch."

The calf's eyes rounded, and it let out a bleat.

Ignoring the creak in his knees and the twinge in his back, he bent down. Today, he'd only chased maybe fifty cows, yet his twenty-eight-year-old bones crackled as if he were sixty. Every weary muscle on his six-foot frame ached, but the poor critter needed tending, and he wouldn't sleep without helping it.

"Gotta clean this. If you cooperate, we'll both get sleep tonight." He tied the rope around a Joshua tree and used his bandana to wipe off the worst of the blood.

Walking to his saddlebag, he grabbed supplies. His canteen clicked against his belt buckle embedded with a quarter-sized garnet. The silver heirloom once symbolized a future filled with happiness. He ran his fingertips over the inlaid stone. Today, the blood-red garnet symbolized the loss of his family ranch.

Ten yards away to the east, a blonde woman gathered wildflowers. Where'd she come from? A lone woman didn't belong in the middle of the desert.

He stepped toward her and waved his hat. "Howdy, miss."

The young lady didn't see him. Her colors faded as her shape became transparent, and she vanished.

"Where'd you go?" He rubbed his eyes. Sagebrush, plenty of sagebrush and nothing else. *Must be seeing things.*

The calf bawled, bringing him back to his task.

"Quit complaining." Holding the dang animal between his legs, he cleaned the cut while thinking about the bonus from tomorrow's roundup. With what he'd saved, it might be enough money to buy a ranch. He applied a generous amount of smelly salve to the calf's leg. "Easy there, we're 'bout done."

By the time he finished, the sun had set. A full moon led him along the trail. Certain dinner would be gone, he snatched jerky from his saddlebag, and took a bite and pretended he was biting into a juicy steak. Pulled out hardtack and pretended he was eating fried potatoes. Pretending never worked.

Thirty minutes later inside his cabin, he stretched out on a goose-feathered mattress and drew his ragged patchwork quilt to his chin. His shin throbbed. Damn calf.

Exhausted, he needed sleep, but his mind whirled. *Check the creek for strays. Remind Ace to ride lead. See if the holding pens are sound. Stop fretting and get some shut eye.*

He counted. "One cow, two cows, three cows—a whole dang herd."

Quit being a fool and go to sleep. He eyeballed the ceiling and counted one million cows.

His eyes closed, and he envisioned the blonde. Why'd she keep popping up, making him question his sanity? Maybe a dozen times in his life, he'd see a vision of a blonde. She was always in the distance, never close enough to see her face. It usually happened when he was overly tired.

He'd obviously been too long without a woman.

It couldn't have been more than an hour, and the old red rooster crowed his greeting. He yanked back the covers, stumbled out of bed, and dressed. What happened to his other boot? It took getting down on his knees to locate the object under the bed.

Slamming the door, he stomped over to the main house in a sleep deprived, cantankerous mood. The already warm morning meant the day would be a scorcher.

"Howdy." From under the eaves by the dining hall entrance, the cook flipped flapjacks on a cast iron stove.

Dusty gave a cordial don't-bother-jawin'-to-me-nod and went inside. A dozen cowboys sat in mismatched chairs and ate at long wooden tables. They jabbered, forking food in their mouths. Full mouths didn't cease their conversing. The men were noisier than a wagon on a frozen road.

He headed for the sideboard, filling his dish with

scrambled eggs, crisp bacon, flapjacks, and fried taters. Holding a cup of thick Arbuckle coffee, he slunk into a vacant chair on the end of a table.

Reynolds and Slick sat in the corner. Their loud voices jangled Dusty's nerves. Reynolds' chuckling turned to snorting. Slick's chortle could pass for an enraged bull.

The ranch owner's nephew on his wife's side, Reynolds, touched the brim of his hat, and called, "Mornin' boss," to Dusty.

Dusty would bet his boots and saddle Reynolds brewed trouble. His sly glares kept Dusty wary. Yesterday, Dusty had found his cinch snipped, making him wonder if the incident had been intentional.

Dusty's friend, Trevor, took the chair next to him. The skinny wrangler had to be pushing forty; still, he could ride and rope like a man in his twenties. "You okay?"

"Yep." His problems were none of the cowboy's concern.

Trevor wore a goofy grin. "Hard to reckon freedom comes tomorrow afternoon."

Dusty smiled. "No cow punching or chores for three days. Can't wait for that room at the Hesperia Hotel." He planned a hot bath, a stiff drink, perhaps the company of a woman.

"Can't stop thinking about the cowboy, Dusty Mann," Mia said, standing next to Birdie at the depot's wide-open platform. Dusty didn't look like a criminal. His eyes seemed bright, not dull like the men on internet mugshots.

"Dusty Mann?" Birdie laughed. "What kind of name is that?"

"Be nice. The poor guy hanged." Mia held her hand against her throat.

Birdie made a pretend noose motion. "Hanged, as in from the highest tree death?"

"Now you're making fun of him."

"If you're interested in cowboys, I'll set you up with one of my brother's friends."

Mia rolled her eyes. "No more blind dates."

"We'll see." Her cousin's smirk meant she'd be persistent. She reached in her purse and handed her a delicate floral tapestry coin purse. "Found this in grandma's attic last week and added three silver dollars to commemorate our trip."

Mia hugged her cousin. "You're so sweet." She tucked the items inside her purse, deciding to check out the coins when they were seated on the train.

Directly in front of her, a barbershop quartet harmonized an old love song. Their red striped vests, straw hats, and handlebar mustaches added to the ambiance.

No surprise, Birdie knew the lyrics.

Auntie Mickie walked up and pulled Mia inside a lavender-scented hug. "I'm glad you moved back."

"Me too." Mia didn't mind housesitting for her grandparents, especially since she didn't have to pay rent for a year. She didn't mind her relatives—but would miss hanging out with her friends in the city.

"Something bugging you?" Auntie Mickie asked.

Darn intuitive aunt.

"Nope." Mia had to fight to keep from clenching her teeth.

"Uncle Al's old west cookout sounded fun," Birdie said. "Why didn't you go with him?"

"Riding horses for hours and sleeping on the hard ground has absolutely no appeal for me." Her aunt fidgeted with the netting on her Knobby hat.

"I'm with Auntie." Mia tugged a capped sleeve down. "Last time I camped, I stepped in a gopher hole and twisted my ankle. Now I'm more into resorts."

"Well, I'd do it. Must've been quite a trip." Her cousin made a wanna-be-a-cowgirl lasso in the air.

Auntie Mickie tapped her pointy black-and-white boots and laughed.

The train's horn blasted from a distance. Voices buzzed. Everyone crowded the gate as Mia edged forward. The steam locomotive chugged, hissing and billowing steam clouds as it stopped.

Birdie posed by one of the car's wheels. "The rims are taller than I am."

Mia grabbed her phone and took a picture. "That's not saying a lot."

Birdie stuck out her tongue.

The conductor flipped open his pocket watch. "Welcome to the California Southern Railroad. You'll find traveling on this fifty-thousand-pound wonder a step back into the year eighteen-ninety."

Dusty may have ridden on a train like this. Birdie was right; Mia had to stop thinking about the darn cowboy.

Auntie Mickie led them up grated metal steps and into the gaming car. Half-a-dozen men in period black duster-coats, tooled leather boots, and dark Stetsons leaned against a mahogany bar, drinking beer out of glass mugs. To her left, gamblers played cards at a felt-covered table. A redheaded man winked at her.

She flashed him a smile, rushed behind her aunt, out the vintage train door, and into the passenger car. A lady held a young girl on her lap; both wore matching periwinkle dresses and bonnets.

Auntie Mickie pointed two rows ahead to a middle-aged woman with tangerine glasses. "Let's sit over by my friend."

Mia took the window seat next to Birdie, facing her aunt.

Birdie crossed her right leg and leaned over to Mia. "Can't wait for the Daggett Western Shindig tomorrow night."

"Remember those crepe-papered high school dances in the gym?" The high school gym where Mia initially danced with her cowboy crush, Craig.

"Sure. They were a blast."

The server handed Mia champagne. She sipped. Bubbles tickled down her throat. A giddiness filled her for the first time in months.

Her cousin lifted her glass and toasted, "To adventures."

After far too many hours staring at her computer screen, Mia was more than ready for an adventure. The whistle blared, and the train jerked forward. She lazed back into the plush seat. A gentle breeze drifted in from the open windows as the car rolled along the tracks. Its wheels clickety-clacked.

"You double-crossing son of a polecat," a raspy voice came from a bearded man, less than a foot from Birdie, blocking the middle of the aisle. He wore a dirty, red-checkered shirt, a weathered cowboy hat, and his lip twisted into a glower.

At the opposite end of the train car, a man, resembling Wild Bill Hickok, fingered the handle of his gun and kept his eyes on his opponent. "It's a mistake to draw first."

The other man pulled out his six-shooter and squeezed the trigger.

Fake gunfire boomed. Wild Bill's opponent fell to the carpet.

Even knowing they were actors, Mia flinched and told her heart to chill. She glanced at Birdie. Her eyes fixed on the still body as her fingernails dug into the seat's padded arm.

The conductor squatted beside the body. "The man's dead!" he shouted to Wild Bill.

"If you don't want to die with your boots on, let that gun lie!" Wild Bill's voice projected the famous line to the audience.

"Bravo." Her cousin whistled, her face shone, and her eyes sparkled. "Wild Bill's hot."

"Probably married," Mia whispered.

The actors stood, bowed, and headed into the next car.

Mia stared out the window. The train rolled past a stand of eucalyptus trees as they wound through the foothills and ascended to a plateau. Creosote bushes and Joshua trees scattered along the dry ground. She found the desert's simplistic beauty calming.

Auntie Mickie pushed her head out her window. "We're climbing the Cajon Pass." The train meandered east and crossed under the freeway. "Summit Valley's over that hill."

Birdie nudged her. "You got any gum?"

Mia moved her valise onto her lap and took out her purse. "In here somewhere." She pulled out a small black box. "I forgot about this." Flipping the lid open, she put the ring on and admired the gemstones. "Got it at the antique shop."

"Let me see." Birdie's green eyes glittered.

Mia lifted her hand up so her cousin could get a look at her purchase.

"Nice."

"The Hesperia Airport's around the bend. Ellen and Sally said they'd be waiting by the tracks." Auntie Mickie pointed. "There they are, right by the bridge."

The metal band felt hot against Mia's finger. She twisted and pulled on the ring, but the thing didn't budge. Her heart raced. "Birdie, do you have lotion … anything to get this ring off? It's burning my finger."

"I'll check."

Mia's vision blurred. Vibrant colors rotated like a hyper kaleidoscope. Dizzy, she shut her eyes.

A whistle shrilled, the train stopped, and her valise thunked to the floor.

She opened her eyes and turned to Birdie. "Hey—" An unknown woman slept in her cousin's place. "What the heck?"

In her aunt's spot, an older man smoked a hand-rolled cigar. An icy wave shivered up her spine. This couldn't be right. The combination of her tight corset and lack of oxygen must've caused her to hallucinate.

The man puffed smoke in her direction. A gray haze curled around her face. Her eyes watered, fumes went up her nostrils, and she coughed.

Fresh air, she needed fresh air. She hurried along the center aisle to an open doorway and stopped, catching her breath.

COWBOY'S CUPID

Cowboy's Cupid

If you enjoyed HER PONY EXPRESS HERO, you might want to read COWBOY'S CUPID from my Love's Magic Series.

A Forbidden Love

When Cupid's arrow accidentally strikes the wrong cowboy, she's supposed to fix her mistake—not fall for the alluring mortal.

Cami Calypso receives her first assignment just in time for the Valentine season. As a newbie Cupid Archer, her life is perfect until her arrow accidentally strikes the wrong man. She has sixty days to secure a job as his housekeeper on a ranch and find the cowboy his soul mate—not keep him for herself.

Rhett Holloway needs a housekeeper and cook.

He doesn't need an adorable blonde to distract him.

He doesn't need her to fix his love life.

But here she is, and he finds her irresistible.

Read the first chapter from COWBOY'S CUPID.

COWBOY'S CUPID CHAPTER 1

The Realm of Cupid's Corner

EVER SINCE THE PINT-SIZE CUPID, Cami Calypso, held a bow, she dreamed of becoming an elite archer like her father. She used to sit on his lap while he told her about his adventures on Earth. He'd been all over the world, promoting love with a special love-potion arrow.

With her town suspended above puffy cumulous clouds, Cami longed for her own chance to slide down a sunbeam and experience Earth for herself. Today, if she wins the Golden Arrow Challenge and secures a spot at the Archery Academy, her wish might come true. Since it was the beginning of January, she'd receive her initial assignment in time for the Valentine's season. The best season of all.

She had to win.

A soft breeze from Lake Aphrodite cooled her face as she furled her wings with shimmering pink hearts. She sucked in a breath of determination. Selected as the first shooter, she had her pick of the four traditional style targets lining the field.

Each target sat on tripod stands precisely three inches from the regulation neon pink line. She knew the ring colors on the target by heart. Golden yellow in the center surrounded by rings of red, blue, and black. Two was her lucky number, so she chose the second target from the right.

As she flew to her spot on the cushy cloud-topped field and stood behind the plum-colored waiting line in the center of Cupid's Stadium, she wiggled her toes inside her satin slippers, stretched her fingers, eyed the yellow center of her target, and silently psyched herself up for a victory.

The championship is mine.

Out of habit, she flipped her braid behind her and glanced sideways at the grandstands. Pink and blue pennants waved. Every family in Cupid's Corner must be out there.

She squared her shoulders and checked out the competition. The teenage girl on her left bounced on her toes. Definitely anxious.

At almost twenty-two, Cami had maturity on her side, but she also knew better than to be overconfident and let down her guard.

Her eyes strayed to her main opponent on her right. Zander Eros. They'd grown up as neighbors. Friends. Since she and Zander were toddlers making fairy dust castles, their families had nudged them together. As they grew older, they frolicked in the lush, grassy meadows where he'd make her bouquets resplendent with poppies, lupines, pansies, lavender, and pink lady slippers. Lately, Zander had been pushing for a romantic relationship. She'd balked, blaming her hesitancy on wanting to secure her career. Both of their mothers hinted about marriage and grandcherubs. Right now. Cami desired neither a husband nor babies.

She reminded herself this wasn't the time to allow her mind to wander, not if she wanted to win. Jitters threatened to undo her tightly controlled resolve.

"Cami Calypso is up first," the announcer called. "She's the daughter of Clark Calypso. I'm sure you're all aware of his three consecutive Golden Arrow wins before the age of eighteen. Let's see if Cami has inherited her father's accuracy."

The announcer might as well say she would never compare to her dad.

With her back to the audience, she took her archer's

stance and nocked the arrow. Breathing in divine oxygen calmed her nervousness. *I've got this.*

Drawing her bowstring, she aimed and released. Her arrow swooshed into the bullseye.

Yes! One down.

Applause followed. Excitement buzzed as she looked toward the stands. Pink flags waved.

Cami gazed up at the majestic snowcapped mountains to the north and thanked the gods for the ideal mid-sixties temperature, not bitter cold like last month.

Her powdered-pink long-sleeved silk gown grazed her knees. The knit stockings kept her legs cozy warm.

"Go Cami! Go Cami!" someone in the audience chanted. Another Cupid in the top bleacher did a flip in the air.

"Nice shot, Cams," Zander said, wearing a metallic gold suit that reminded her of a foil wrapped candy bar. He gave her a confident I've-got-this-bagged smile and released his arrow. No surprise, seconds later Zander's arrow zipped into the golden center. He rarely missed. He wasn't her only competition, but it suddenly seemed that way.

A male Cupid, two targets over from her, hit an inch above the mark and groaned.

The other female contestant's tip struck the middle.

It was Cami's turn again. She shut out the noise and

concentrated. Her second arrow sailed dead center into the bullseye.

The crowd cheered.

Zander took his shot.

She silently said, "Please miss." He didn't need this victory. Two years ago, he attended the Archery Academy. She deserved this chance.

Naturally, Zander made his mark. Cocky, he blew a kiss to the crowd.

The other female archer shifted back and forth on her feet. The skittish Cupid's arrow missed center, the second red ring, and stuck into the edge of the third. Her error took her out of the final round. The poor girl's eyes misted with tears.

After making a similar error, an error that cost Cami a win in last year's finals, she sympathized with the girl. It had been a devastating blow to Cami's ego, and her father barely spoke to her for a full month. When he did, he had never called her a disappointment, but she could see it in his eyes.

This time things would be different. She hoped anyway.

The next guy missed the center by a good two inches, and shouted, "Cursed Cyclops!"

Cami laughed on the inside. She had been taught to watch her language in public, but she could totally relate.

"Tied for first, Zander Eros and Cami Calypso," the announcer called. "Now for our favorite part of this exhibition. These young folks move on to the final round with virtual human targets." He pushed a lever, and the standing targets disappeared.

A grassy park, complete with sidewalks and trees, replaced the cloudy ground. Six animatronic humans appeared where the targets had been. The moving people shone with a translucent quality. They walked in clusters, their hearts twinkling, their heads bobbing, their steps unpredictable.

She couldn't lose to Zander again.

Okay, I can beat him like I did last fall. I just have to shut out everything around me.

"Cami you're up first," the announcer called. "Remember, all three shots must be done while you are in the air, or you're disqualified."

Breathe. Think about the hours of practice. Hundreds of perfect shots. Breathe. Tune out the audience. Breathe.

She knew the drill and shot up in the air several yards, slowing her wings to a rhythmic flutter.

A woman strolled on the sidewalk next to a man holding her hand. With most humans, their aura appeared with heightened emotions. His pale-yellow aura meant he was the target.

She stopped and faced the man.

Perfect, they had eye contact.

Holding her bow, Cami aimed and released.

A brilliant heart flickered on the front of the man's shirt.

One down, two to go.

Somebody shouted from the stadium bleachers, "Go, Cami!" Her young and carefree sister in the second row gave her a thumbs up. Unlike Cami who normally braided her hair, her sister, Affinity, preferred her blonde tresses loose and blowing in the wind.

With a renewed sense of determination, Cami spotted her next target, a couple glaring at one another. The scenario seemed almost too easy. They faced each other, the woman with her hands on her hips. Cami circled above them three times, cognizant they could change course in an instant. Just like she'd figured, the girl turned away. Her boyfriend with the yellow aura grabbed her arm and forced her to look at him. Three-sixtying around the couple, she notched the arrow, drew, aimed, and released. Swoosh. The tip embedded into the heart on the human's shirt and it flashed a red light.

The applause made her confidence soar. She might actually win the competition. In the stands, her mother waited on the edge of her seat with her fingers crossed.

She centered in on the last couple walking a virtual dog. The woman kneeled to pet the animal. Cami's shot was tricky. If the woman stood, Cami might hit the animal.

Patience had never been her strong point, but to win this contest she must show restraint. The man grabbed the leash from the woman. "Give Duke back!" the woman yelled facing her boyfriend. Cami aimed carefully, checked that everything lined up, and released. A heart glowed on the woman's shirt.

Cami had made all three shots. Spectators cheered as she gracefully floated down to the ground. She wasn't sure who yelled louder, her mother or her best friends, Belle and Serenity.

Zander stood next to her. "Way to go, Cams."

His one-syllable nickname, Cams, made her feel mundane and boring. She shook off the negative senti-ment, and said, "Thanks."

It was his turn. The first two arrows hit their mark. Zander released his third arrow. Magical dust scattered from the feathers as the arrow whooshed across the field. A glittery line of gold added pizzazz.

"Show off," Cami muttered under her breath, not at all appreciative of his stunt.

His arrow hit the man's shoulder. Crazy, weird, uncharacteristic.

No sparkling heart.

He missed.

She'd won, she'd really won. Adrenaline hummed

through her veins like Poseidon racing across the ocean. She'd won the coveted Aphrodite's Golden Arrow, wresting the championship from Zander.

Her mother hurried up to her, happiness filling her shimmering eyes. "Sweetie, I'm proud of you."

Her sister gave her a high-heaven hand slap. "Knew you'd win."

"Too bad your father's judging the ten-year-olds' meet and missed your stellar performance," Mom said. "He did promise to watch the live video feed on his Cupitron watch."

Mother tended to cover for her dad, trying to keep peace in their family. The truth was her father's absence proved he still hadn't gotten over last year's loss in the finals.

Her roommate, Belle, hugged her. "You were spectacular."

"Awesome shooting." Serenity made a three-way embrace.

Attending the Academy, she'd fulfill her dreams, dreams she'd had since she first held a bow.

Zander stepped in front of her, donning a weird grin. "Good match. Can't believe you beat me."

"Me neither."

He winked, the kind of wink that felt too personal. "You're gonna love the Academy. Once you graduate, I'm sure we'll do assignments together."

Wait a minute! "Did you intentionally lose? You know I'd never accept a win that wasn't true." The idea had her fuming. She was an excellent marksman. After countless hours practicing for this event, she deserved the victory. It didn't set right with her that he may have rigged his shot. This made her wonder about his motives. Did he figure once she had two or three Earthly travels out of the way, she'd be ready for a serious relationship?

"I can't believe you're asking me that, Cams." He looked her in the eye. "I wouldn't do that for you or anyone else."

Since his eye didn't twitch. His eye tended to twitch when he lied, so she took his words at face value and felt bad. "Sorry."

"You've worked hard. Revel in your success."

"I will." She stared at Zander. He seemed to be her best choice as far as suitors were concerned. Handsome, talented, and quite a catch. Why did she feel like something was missing?

The group fluttered toward the square administration building; its style was similar to the Parthenon in Greece. Two young assistants flew between the outer columns of the porch and trumpeted with golden horns.

The captain's wings flickered with red and white lights as he floated down to center stage. "Would all the archery contestants please come forward?"

The heart emblem on Cami's wrist sparkled in a rainbow prism. Unfurling her wings to stretch out on each side, she flew up the stairs and took her spot with Zander and the other archer.

"We've had a thrilling contest today," the captain said with an infectious grin. "Now for our winners."

Cami found herself smiling.

"The Bronze Arrow goes to Vanessa Venus."

A cute blonde fluttered, accepted her arrow, and waved to the audience. Cheers abounded.

"The Silver Arrow goes to Alexander Eros."

Zander accepted his arrow and added it to the two golden ones already in his quiver.

"Miss Calypso, please step forward."

Excited, she held the sides of her flowing silver gown, lifted her chin, and curtsied.

"On behalf of our council, I award Cami Calypso with Aphrodite's Golden Arrow. Please kneel." The captain anointed her, touching the top of her head with ambrosia from the arrow's tip.

Her heart filled with jubilation.

"I'd like to congratulate all the contestants for their excellent marksmanship." The captain shook each of the archers' hands and excused everyone, while motioning for Cami to stay.

A young student gave the captain a scroll, and he unrolled the glittery parchment.

She'd waited so long to be sent to the Academy.

"In recognition for your archery accomplishment, the council hereby invites Cami Calypso to attend the Academy of Archers."

Yes! She restrained herself, holding in the urge to shout at the top of her lungs. Instead, she waved to the crowd.

"Classes shall begin two days hence."

"Thank you, captain. I am pleased and honored to be selected."

He nodded. "Once again, let's give a round of applause for Miss Calypso."

Unbelievable. These cheers were for her.

The captain pivoted on the heels of his white leather boots and exited the ceremonial stage.

Amazing. Her first Earthly assignment would be in the Valentine's season. Breathless, she dashed down the steps.

She couldn't wait for new adventures far from this community.

Cedar Springs, California

. . .

THANKS TO A COUPLE of hours attempting to break a cantankerous stallion, Rhett Holloway needed a good stiff drink. His back spasmed, his shoulders throbbed, and nearly every muscle in his twenty-nine-year-old body ached.

He limped into the rundown Last Call Saloon. A scratchy song drifted from the jukebox as old as the building. "Can't Help Falling in Love" crooned, sung by Elvis. A love song. Ugh! How could someone pay to hear this miserable drivel?

Three or four yards across the room, he spotted his friend's blond hair at the bar and walked toward Ace. Something pink lay on the scuffed floor, and he picked up a woman's Stetson. Pink. His ex wore a pink hat similar to this one that painful Valentine's night two years ago.

He threw the lame hat on top of the long mahogany bar and slid into the barstool next to his high school buddy.

"Trying to change your image?" Ace taunted as he motioned to the hat.

"Actually, I brought it for you."

The Stetson's heart-shaped centerpiece sparkled with rhinestones. Hearts reminded him that his family's Valentine's Day party would be in two weeks. To avoid dealing with well-intended meddling, he'd hang out with the cute brunette working at his neighbor's ranch.

The bearded bartender wiped down the counter. "Want a draft?"

"You bet. Make it lager." From a side room, pool balls clacked. Somebody groaned, another person broke out in laughter.

Handed a mug, Rhett took a swig of the dark brew. He overheard a lady's distressed voice at a table behind him. "You can't work on Valentine's Day."

"I have no choice," a man answered.

Rhett considered Valentine's Day another way for florists and jewelry stores to make a buck.

"Rough day?" Ace asked. "You get that horse broke yet?"

"Not sure who's breaking who." Rhett laughed. "Think it might be time to change professions. Must be nice to stay home and get paid to play video games."

"Hey, I'm a programmer." His stocky friend punched Rhett's sore shoulder.

Rhett winced and held back a moan. Asshole stallion.

"You okay?"

"I'll live."

Ace motioned the bartender for another beer. "Want one? I'm buying."

"Sure." Rhett removed his hat, set it next to the ridiculous pink one, and asked the bartender, "Any idea who might've lost this?"

"My guess it's one of the out-of-towners playing pool."

"I noticed those chicks when I walked in. They're hot." Ace put on his white Stetson. "You up for a game of pool?"

Rhett shifted so he could watch a leggy redhead. She leaned over the pool table, her long hair fell forward as she positioned the shot. She must've sensed his eyes on her because she glanced over her shoulder and smiled in his direction. He raised his glass. The motion made his shoulder twinge.

"You comin'?"

"Not this time." Rhett took another drink.

Ace shrugged. "Mind if I try 'n' find the owner?" He snatched the pink hat and twirled it on his finger.

"Go right ahead." He watched his friend chat with the ladies. Usually, Rhett would have joined him, flirted with the women, and let the night develop, but his aching muscles kept him rooted to his seat.

The redhead donned the pink hat, reminding him of that fateful Valentine's Day, and ruined any attraction he had for her.

BOOKS

Romance Novels by Niki Mitchell
Time Travel Romance
TIME TO SAVE THE COWBOY
TIME FOR CHANGE
TIME FOR LOVE

Love's Magic Series
COWBOY'S CUPID
REBEL'S CUPID
FIREBRAND'S CUPID

Stand-alone Romance
HER PONY EXPRESS HERO
LOVE'S HIGH TIDE

Children's Books by Niki Mitchell
KURIOUS KATZ
KURIOUS KATZ AND THE BIG MOVE
KURIOUS KATZ AND THE PLAY DAY
KURIOUS KATZ AND THE NEW FRIEND
KURIOUS KATZ AND THE BIRTHDAY PARTY
KURIOUS KATZ AND THE HALLOWEEN
COSTUMES
KURIOUS KATZ AND THE CHRISTMAS TREE
KURIOUS KATZ AND THE BEST CHRISTMAS
EVER
FOSTER CATS: ARTEMIS AND HER SNEAKY
BROTHER HERCULUES
KURIOUS KATZ AND THE FOURTH OF JULY
KURIOUS KATZ AND THE VALENTINE SURPRISE
KURIOUS KATZ AND THE SNICKERDOODLE
STORY
PRECIOUS PUPS: BREEZY GETS ADOPTED

ABOUT THE AUTHOR

Niki Mitchell writes children's books along with contemporary fantasy and historical time-travel romance. She was born in Chicago, Illinois, and moved to Whittier, California in first grade. With a houseful of books and a local library located a few short blocks, her love of reading began at a young age.

Married for over thirty years and a romantic at heart, she enjoys writing about strong female characters in unusual settings. When she isn't playing with her cats, she loves reading, taking walks, water aerobics, photography, and traveling.

Dear Readers,

Thank you for reading HER PONY EXPRESS EXPRESS HERO.

I hope you enjoyed my story as much as I enjoyed writing it. Won't you please consider leaving a review? Even just a few words will help others decide if the book is right for them.

Best regards and thank you in advance.

Niki J. Mitchell

I look forward to hearing from my readers.

Visit me at https://nikimitchell.weebly.com/

Follow me on FaceBook at <u>Author Niki Mitchell</u>

Twitter: <u>Niki Mitchell@NikiMitchell7</u>

Instagram: NikiJMitchellAuthor

www.ingramcontent.com/pod-product-compliance
Lightning Source LLC
Chambersburg PA
CBHW070615310726
48982CB00001B/86